The ONE NIGHT STAND *before* CHRISTMAS

T.K. LEIGH WRITING AS
TRACY LEIGH

THE ONE NIGHT STAND BEFORE CHRISTMAS

ALL RIGHTS RESERVED. Excluding short, selected passages quoted for review or educational purposes, this work may not be reproduced, transmitted, or illegally distributed in any form or by any means currently available or available in the future, including but not limited to electronic, photographic, audio, and video reproduction, in whole or in part, for free or for sale, without express written permission from the publisher and author.

AI RESTRICTION: The author expressly prohibits any entity from using any part of this publication, including text and graphics, for purposes of training artificial intelligence (AI) technologies to generate text or graphics, including without limitation technologies that are capable of generating works in the same style or genre as this publication.

The author reserves all rights to license uses of this work for generative AI training and development of machine learning language models.

Unauthorized duplication and distribution of this book to others infringes the rights of the legal copyright holder and is strictly forbidden and a violation of international copyright law.

This is a work of fiction. Names, characters, places, and incidents either are the product of the author's imagination and any resemblance to actual persons, living or dead, business establishments, events, or locales is entirely coincidental or, if an actual place, are used fictitiously. The author acknowledges the trademarked status and trademark owners of various products referenced in this work of fiction, which have been used without permission. The use of these trademarks is not sponsored, associated, or endorsed by the trademark owner.

Published by Carpe Per Diem Publishing, Inc

Cover Design: Cat Head Media, Inc.

Cover assets © 2025

Illustrated stock used under license from Qamber Designs

Copyright © 2025
All rights reserved.

For a full list of all of Tracy's books, including recommended reading order, please visit her website:

www.tracyleigh.com

Books and reading order for her spicy billionaire romance alter ego, T.K. Leigh, can be found here:

www.tkleighauthor.com

Some of the author's books may contain content that could be triggering for sensitive readers. For a full list of content warnings for each book and/or series, please scan the code below.

For exclusive sales and excerpts,
sign up for Tracy Leigh's VIP list!

https://www.tracyleighbooks.com/subscribe

Or scan the code below

For the readers who believe age is just a number, Christmas is best with a side of spice, and bad ideas make the best stories.

ONE

Claire

"I'm so sorry, Parker," I rush out as I pace in front of the window overlooking the city of Boston that's covered with a thick blanket of snow. And there's even more falling at a steady clip.

Normally, I'd love everything about this. The tranquility of the city as snow falls. The crispness in the air. Watching kids build snowmen.

Not right now, though.

Not when there's so much I need to do back home.

"I tried to get an earlier flight once I learned about the snowstorm, but everyone had the same idea. I'll do everything I can to get on the first flight out, but—"

"Claire," my boss interrupts in a gentle but firm tone, "it's not your fault Logan Airport turned into a snow globe. You can't control the weather."

"But it's almost Thanksgiving," I reply, filled with guilt over the prospect of being away from Holley Ridge for a night longer than we originally planned.

The conference I attended this week was everything I hoped it would be and more. Panels on winter marketing trends, guest engagement, influencer packages. But the storm grounded every flight out of Boston until tomorrow morning at the earliest.

"The Christmas festival is just weeks away. And with all the additional events, I—"

"The only thing you need to worry about is whether to order white or red wine at the hotel bar."

"I can start batching some content ahead of time," I assure Parker so she doesn't have to worry about me falling behind. "Can probably put together some promos for the baking competition we've added."

"Claire."

"Just a few videos and graphics. I can also—"

"Claire Thomas," Parker interjects, her voice demanding, causing me to snap my mouth shut. When she speaks again, her tone is softer. Lighter. "You've been working nonstop on this for weeks. *Months*. You need to take a break. Trust me."

I groan, pinching the bridge of my nose. "You sound like my sister."

"Because she's right. I used to be like you. Working every waking moment to prove to everyone I could do it."

I part my lips to argue, but she cuts me off.

"If you even think about opening your laptop again tonight, you're fired."

"It's the least I should do since I'm stuck here for another night."

"No. It's the *last* thing you should do. Go to the hotel bar. Order a drink. Flirt with a stranger. Live a little."

"Flirting with strangers isn't my strong suit," I admit.

"Neither is relaxing apparently. Consider this a learning opportunity. After all, you know what Grandma Estelle says, don't you?"

"I'm not sure I want to know," I mutter under my breath, all too familiar with how eccentric our small town's octogenarian can be.

"According to her, creativity spikes after a dopamine hit. And there's no bigger dopamine hit than some sexy times with an attractive man."

I should be mortified the woman who is technically my boss is all but encouraging me to have a one-night stand while away on a business trip she paid for.

But Parker's always been more than just a boss. Being from a town as small as Sycamore Falls, everyone tends to be more like extended family, Parker included.

"So go. Have some fun. Step out of your comfort zone for once. That's a direct order."

She hangs up before I can protest, leaving me alone with my overactive brain and the weight of just wanting to prove that, despite being only twenty-four, I can handle the marketing of a popular inn and premier wedding destination, particularly during their popular Christmas festival that draws thousands of people every year.

I'm more than aware Parker took a risk in giving me this job when she could have hired someone with so much more experience.

I don't want her to regret her decision.

Which is why instead of going downstairs to the bar, I open my laptop.

Almost instantly, my phone buzzes.

PARKER:

I can feel you working. STOP. Go have a drink. Flirt. Be twenty-four. Work will always be there. The handsome stranger you might meet won't.

I laugh at how well she knows me.

I can't deny that a glass of wine *does* sound good.

So despite everything I *should* be doing right now, I follow my boss' order and close my laptop.

The lobby is straight out of a holiday movie. Twinkling fairy lights wrap around the exposed beams overhead. A towering fir tree glows with gold and red ornaments. Garlands of pine drape over the mantle of the oversized fireplace, filling the space with the crisp scent of evergreen. There's even soft instrumental carols playing in the background, subtle enough not to annoy the non-holiday crowd.

My marketing brain immediately starts cataloging everything. The balance between opulence and comfort. The warm lighting. The curated scents.

But then I catch myself.

No working, Claire. Remember?

But turning off my brain is like trying to stop a freight train. Hopefully, a glass of wine will help.

The bar is nestled in the corner, a cozy blend of historic charm and modern sophistication. Brass sconces cast warm pools of light over wooden barstools. Glass shelves gleam behind the bar, displaying bottles like trophies. A fireplace crackles quietly in the corner, surrounded by low tables where votive candles flicker gently beside half-full glasses.

I take a seat at the bar and order a glass of cabernet. The bartender returns quickly with my wine. After snapping a photo of the glass against the elegant bar top, I send it to Parker.

ME:

Happy?

PARKER:

So proud. Now drink up.

I lift the glass, letting the familiar aroma invade my senses before taking a sip. Warmth trickles through me — berries, oak, the faintest hint of spice. I close my eyes and let myself enjoy it for two whole seconds before someone slides into the seat beside me.

"You look familiar."

His voice is smooth. *Too* smooth.

I glance at him and recognize him instantly. Not for anything good, though.

I overheard him earlier bragging to a group of men about how conferences are "a prime hunting ground."

His eyes rake over me. Slowly. Hungrily.

"You were at the conference, weren't you?"

I nod politely and shift away, hoping the chill in my expression is enough of a hint.

It's not.

He leans closer, taking a sip of his drink. "Crazy weather, huh? Guess we're all stuck tonight. Could be worse ways to pass the time, though." He leers at me again, his gaze landing squarely on my chest.

"I'm actually waiting for someone," I lie.

"Then I'll keep you company until they show up." He grins wider, inching into my space yet again. "Maybe convince you to ditch whoever you're meeting for me."

His hand grazes my knee. There's a faint indentation where a wedding ring usually sits.

"I don't think so."

"Oh, come on." He moves closer, invading even more of my space. His breath reeks of alcohol and fried food. "We're all stranded here another night. May as well make the most of it. I'll make it worth your while."

I inwardly groan. Why do all men think they're God's gift to women? That just because they show a modicum of interest, we'll happily spread our legs?

That may work for other women, but not me.

"I told you. I—"

"I believe the lady told you she wasn't interested."

The voice is low and lethal, smooth as velvet but laced with danger. I turn just as a tall figure steps between us, forcing the creep to pull away from me.

"Who the fuck are you?"

"Someone you don't want to test," the man murmurs just loud enough for him to hear, an air of confidence and control about him. "If I were you, I'd apologize to the lady, then leave."

There's a quiet weight to his words, the kind that comes from someone who's ended fights with a single move. His body radiates restraint, but only barely.

"We were just talking. I—"

"I said to apologize and leave."

Several seconds pass as the two men glare at each other. Finally, the creep stands from his chair.

"Fine," he bites out, downing the rest of his drink and heading toward the elevators.

"I believe you're forgetting something," the man calls after him.

The creep stops in his tracks, confused at first. The suit-clad man simply widens his stance, the threat unmistakable.

"Sorry," the creep mutters.

"I think you can do better."

The creep pins me with a glare, obviously hating to be put in his place. He's probably never experienced it before. But the man won't back down. Instead, he crosses his arms over his broad chest, making him appear even more threatening.

"I'm sorry for not listening."

The man looks my way.

It's the first time I've seen his face. He's older. Distinguished. Dark eyes. Sharp jaw. A bit of scruff, like he didn't bother shaving because he doesn't feel the need to impress anyone. His suit jacket is expensive, and something about the controlled strength and quiet dominance in his body language screams authority.

"Are you satisfied with his apology?"

The deep timbre of his voice causes an unexpected shiver to roll through me, but I push it down and nod. "Yeah. Sure."

The man turns back to the creep. "*Now* you're free to go."

The creep doesn't hesitate. He spins around, muttering under his breath, and disappears into an elevator.

Once the doors close, I release a long breath, taking a much-needed sip of wine.

"Sorry if I overstepped," the man offers after a beat. "I just don't like seeing women being taken advantage of. There are assholes everywhere."

"You're right about that," I retort with a roll of my eyes. "I appreciate you stepping in."

He nods once, then gestures toward my half-empty glass. "Let me buy you another."

"Shouldn't I offer to buy *you* one?"

He quirks a brow. "We're already negotiating. I like that." He moves to the vacant seat beside me but doesn't sit, unlike its previous occupant. "May I?"

My eyes lock on his. A part of me thinks I should thank him again for his help, then insist I have work to do. It's not a complete lie. I *do* have work to do. Another glass of wine will make that challenging.

But Parker's words choose this moment to replay in my head, telling me to live a little. Since starting this job, it's been my focus. I can't even remember the last time I went out for drinks.

So despite the laundry list of things I need to get done, I give the handsome stranger a smile.

"I'd like that."

TWO

Declan

I signal the bartender for another round of drinks, then shift toward the stunning brunette at my side.

The stunning, *younger* brunette.

This is the last thing I should be doing.

Once the jerk who'd been bothering her left, I should have said goodbye and gone back to my room, like a responsible man with a mountain of work and a hell of a lot on his mind.

But I didn't.

There's something about her that caught my attention the second she walked into the bar.

Or maybe I just needed a distraction. Someone to

help keep my mind off everything… Especially the news I learned today.

"I'm Claire, by the way." She extends her hand toward me.

"Declan."

"Declan," she repeats as I wrap my hand around hers.

Soft. Delicate. Warm.

I almost don't want to let go.

But I do.

"Thanks again for the rescue," she says as the bartender sets her fresh wine onto the counter with a light clink. "Though I had it handled."

"I'm sure you did," I agree.

But I know guys like him. Entitled. Arrogant. The type who treat the word "no" like a challenge instead of a refusal.

I've been around enough of them in my life — military, law firms, country clubs. It's always the same. They think the world owes them something because they showed up.

I can tolerate a lot of shit. I've had to. But a man disrespecting a woman?

That's where I draw the line.

That prick's lucky I didn't break his fucking hand. I *really* wanted to.

"So tell me," Claire begins, cutting through the

silence. Her voice is light and playful. "What exactly are you drinking to forget?"

"Drinking to forget?" I echo.

"Exactly."

"Who says I'm drinking to forget?" I smirk, though there's no real humor behind it. "Maybe I'm here to pass the time."

She tilts her head, studying me in a way that feels invasive. Like she's stripping me bare, seeing things I've worked hard to keep buried. It's unsettling.

And yet I don't look away.

"I don't buy it," she says at last, a slow smile playing across her mouth. "You don't seem the type."

I lift a brow. "And what type do I seem like?"

"Brooding," she answers without a moment's hesitation. "Probably good at giving orders. Not great at taking them. Terrible at relaxing. Emotionally constipated. But..." She lets her gaze drag lazily over my fingers wrapped around my glass as I lift the bourbon to my mouth to mask my reaction over how accurate she is. "Excellent with your hands."

"You learned all that from talking to me for a few minutes?"

"I'm very efficient," she deadpans.

"You forgot judgmental."

"Everyone's judgmental, whether they admit it or not," she says cheerfully. "But don't worry. I balance it out with great legs and a winning personality."

My eyes drift to her crossed legs, left exposed in a slim pencil skirt. They're long and smooth… Impossible to ignore. She catches me admiring them and grins.

"Busted," she taunts.

God, this woman is something else. So full of life. And so damn beautiful. Dark waves of hair tumbling around her shoulders. Bright green eyes that don't miss a thing. And enough curves to scramble a man's better judgment.

Especially mine.

"If you're not drinking to forget, what brings you here?" Her gaze floats over me in curiosity.

"Work."

She waves that off with a flick of her hand. "Not to Boston. *Here*." She taps the bar. "This place. This moment."

"This moment?" I repeat.

"Exactly."

"I guess I was looking for quiet," I respond after a beat. "Or maybe a distraction."

Her smile softens, her eyes sparkling in the low light. "Rough day?"

I could lie. I could dodge. But something in the way she looks at me, open and interested but not pushing, makes me want to tell her the truth.

"I received some news today." I swirl the ice in my glass, watching it clink and spin. "The kind that changes things. Or at least makes you question the last two decades of your life."

I don't say more. I'm not ready to. I'm still wrapping my head around the fact that I have a son I never knew existed. A full-grown man with a life, with questions, and I have nothing but regrets to give him.

"Want to talk about it?" she asks.

"No."

She nods in understanding as another silence settles between us. But it only lasts a matter of seconds before she continues her interrogation.

"Do you always make a habit of rescuing women from creepy guys in bars when you're running from your feelings?"

"I'm not running."

"Denial, then."

I lean in close enough that our knees almost brush. Close enough to smell the wine on her breath. Close enough to see her pulse thrum in her neck.

"Careful, Claire. You keep poking at me, you might not like what you unleash."

"Promise?"

Christ. She's dangerous.

She's everything I shouldn't want.

Everything I can't seem to look away from.

"What about you?" I ask, needing to change the subject. "Do you make a habit out of having a drink with older men you meet in hotel bars?"

She lifts a shoulder, unbothered. "Only the ones with devastating jawlines who flirt with younger women hoping to forget whatever's eating them up inside."

I bring my glass to my lips. "Care to help with that?"

She smiles, slow and knowing. "I think I already am."

She's right. I haven't thought about the test results in ten minutes. Haven't thought about the time I lost or the fact that somewhere out there is a young man trying to understand why his father never came looking for him.

Right now, all I can think about is the curve of her mouth. The spark in her eyes. The slow, simmering heat building between us, getting hotter with every breath.

I came down here to forget, even for a little while.

But maybe the antidote to what I'm feeling isn't at the bottom of a bourbon glass.

Maybe it's sitting next to me.

THREE

Declan

The walk toward the elevators feels longer than it should. With every step, every brush of Claire's arm against mine, the tension in my body winds tighter and tighter, like a coil ready to snap.

Her perfume teases me with each measured inhale. Warm, soft, with a hint of something floral and sweet. She bumps into me lightly, laughing as she tells me about a woman named Grandma Estelle from her hometown who, at eighty-something years young, has a fascination with alien erotica and will tell anyone who will listen about her current read.

I pretend not to notice how the sound of her laughter curves down my spine, or how the heat from her skin seeps through my clothes, settling beneath my ribs.

I shouldn't be walking her to her room. I should have said goodnight at the bar. Hell, I should have said goodnight after one drink. But one turned into two, which I drank slowly so that I had an excuse to linger in her presence a little longer.

We spent the past several hours talking about anything that popped into our heads. Or, more appropriately, anything that popped into Claire's head. I didn't do much talking, but I didn't mind. I liked listening to her voice. Watching her mouth move. She was the distraction I didn't know I needed tonight.

The lobby is mostly empty at this late hour, the click of Claire's heels on the marble floor the only sound. I press the elevator button, keeping my hands jammed into my pockets so I don't do something stupid.

Like reach for her.

Pull her closer.

See if she tastes as sweet as she smells.

Before I can allow my thoughts to run away, the elevator doors slide open and we step inside.

The space feels smaller than it should.

Tighter.

Hotter.

Claire leans against the far wall, her gaze lazily tracking me as I press the button for her floor. She doesn't speak, but she doesn't have to. That look in her eyes — teasing, curious, dangerous — says enough.

I focus on the numbers above the door, watching them change slowly. *Too* slowly.

Every second is a silent dare, every heartbeat a temptation.

Younger women have never been a problem before.

Hell, they made things easier. Women fresh out of college aren't looking for a future. They want fun. A night. A distraction. And that's all I've ever been good for.

But everything's different now that I have a son who's not much older than the women I typically spend the night with.

Hell, he's probably not much older than Claire.

The thought punches me right in the ribs, edged with guilt and regret.

When the elevator slides to a stop on her floor and the doors open once more, I let her step off first, trying to look anywhere but at her.

But when I catch the sway of her hips as she walks, it's damn near impossible. I can feel my heartbeat increase with every step we take toward her room, the silence in the hallway deafening with the tension building between us.

"This is me," she whispers, slowing her steps and

turning to face me. Her smile is soft, sleepy, but there's something behind it. Something that hits like a match struck in the dark. "Thanks for walking me back."

"Of course." I nod, shifting from foot to foot.

Say goodnight, Declan. Turn around. Walk away.

That's what I should do.

But I don't.

Instead, I inch closer.

Close enough to see the faint flush on her cheeks. The gold flecks in her green eyes. The slight part of her lips as she looks at me like she's not afraid of what might happen next.

Like she's *desperate* for what might happen next.

I am, too.

My hands ache to touch her. My body physically burns with it, my cock throbbing with a hunger I haven't experienced in years.

Why now?

Why this woman?

Why tonight?

"Go inside, Claire," I say, my voice rougher than I intend. "Before I do something we'll both regret."

The corner of her mouth curls in a slow, dangerous smile. "Who says I'll regret it?"

Fuck.

My whole body goes rigid, fighting a battle I fear I'm about to lose.

"Go inside," I repeat, pleading with her to do as I ask.

But she doesn't move.

Neither do I.

The air between us is electric with all the things I want to do to her. All the ways I want to taste and touch and claim her.

When I'm not sure I can take another second of this tension, she finally turns toward the door, holding her keycard up to the lock. It beeps, and she steps inside.

But just before she closes the door, she glances back. Our eyes catch. Hold. And I see it.

The want.

The invitation.

The promise.

I want to accept. Want to push into her room and lose myself in her.

But I don't, increasing the distance even more.

Our eyes remain locked on each other as she slowly closes the door, the sound seeming to echo in the hallway.

I let out a long breath and drag a hand through my hair. My legs feel like lead as I turn back toward the elevators.

This is for the best.

My life just got much more complicated than I

anticipated. I don't need to add yet another complication to the mix.

And Claire has complication written all over her.

But that doesn't stop me from pausing in my tracks when I hear the soft click of a door opening again. It could be someone else. There are dozens of rooms on this floor.

I know it's her door.

I feel it.

I feel *her*.

My pulse gradually kicking up, I turn around, the electricity in the air cracking like a damn live wire.

Claire stands just outside her room, her gaze trained on me like I'm the only thing she sees.

For what feels like an eternity, neither of us moves or speaks.

We just stare.

And watch.

And want.

Then something inside me snaps, and I mutter, "Screw it."

My legs move before my brain's had a chance to catch up, long, fast strides eating up the distance between us.

I cup her cheek with one hand, my other settling low on her waist as I back her into the room, the thud of the door slamming closed echoing behind me.

"Are you sure this is what you want?" I rasp as I press her against the wall, my chest heaving.

"You wouldn't be here if I didn't want you to be." Her reply is breathless. Eager. Wanton.

My gaze drops to her mouth, then the rapid rise and fall of her chest. The way she looks at me rips away the last layer of control I've been clinging to.

Still, I try.

"I'm too old for you."

"Age is just a number." She smirks, hoisting herself on her toes, her lips so close to mine. "Why should we deprive ourselves of this because of a few years between us?"

"It's more than just a few years, Claire."

"You're attracted to me, aren't you?" she says in a husky voice that completely undoes me, especially when it's accompanied by her fingertips trailing down my chest, stopping just shy of my belt.

My cock throbs even more.

"God, yes," I exhale.

She leans in again, her lips barely an inch from mine. "And I'm ridiculously attracted to you. So stop overthinking this, Declan. One night. That's all this is."

"One night," I repeat.

Her lips part, as if about to offer me more promises or assurances. But I don't need them. I just need her.

Without wasting another second, I crush my mouth against hers.

FOUR

Claire

There's nothing gentle about the way Declan kisses. It's hungry. Commanding. Like a man starved who's finally taking what he's been denying himself for far too long. And God, I feel it.

Every inch of me sparks to life under his touch. I don't even care about the needy whimpers that fall from my throat or the fact that my breath might taste like the lobster roll I had for dinner.

All I care about is this.

Him.

The way his mouth moves over mine. Like he's lost all control and doesn't care if he takes me down with him.

My fingers tangle in the fabric of his shirt, clutching it like I need something to anchor me to this world. To him. My skin buzzes where his body brushes mine, all hard lines and heat, his hand gripping my hip as if he doesn't want to let go.

And I don't want him to.

He tastes like whiskey and lust and something darker. Something that coils low in my belly and makes my thighs clench.

This isn't me.

I don't do this.

I don't invite strangers into my room. Don't flirt with men at hotel bars. Don't kiss men I barely know, especially ones I'll never see again.

But there's something about Declan that's been undoing me from the moment I laid eyes on him. As if some part of me recognizes something in him. Something bruised and jagged and aching.

Like me.

And if this kiss is any indication, surrendering to him might be the best bad decision I've ever made.

After all, Parker told me to go flirt with a stranger. I'm just following my boss' orders.

Declan's hand slides up the curve of my body, his touch leaving a scorched trail in its wake, erasing every thought from my mind. Except for him. When his fingers brush the line of my jaw, I can feel his restraint. Like he's holding himself back, albeit barely. But I don't want him to hold back.

If we only have one night together, I want him to let go. Give me everything he's willing to give.

I want him to completely wreck me.

I break the kiss first, but I don't move far. My mouth hovers over his, hungry for more.

"What the hell was that?" he rasps, almost in awe.

I lift my eyes toward his, my lips still tingling, heart pounding far too loud in my chest.

God.

No one has ever looked at me like this. Like they feel me in their bones. Like I just shook something loose they didn't know existed.

"Well," I murmur, brushing my lips against his stubbled jaw, "when a boy really likes a girl, they kiss."

He laughs, and the sound does something to me. It's low and rough and full of life.

I didn't think he could get any sexier, but that delicious rumble does it. I want to hear it more. Want to be the reason he laughs.

But then something shifts.

His smile fades, and his expression darkens. Not cold. Not cruel.

Intense.

Hungry.

Predatory.

It strips me bare in the best way possible.

"Do you know what else a boy and girl do when they really like each other?" he asks in a gruff voice that sets my insides on fire.

"What's that?"

His hips press into mine, slow and deliberate. I feel it. I feel *him*.

Hard. Thick. Unapologetic.

A shock of heat bolts through me, and I gasp, my body arching instinctively.

"They fuck, Claire."

His mouth finds the crook of my neck, lips brushing my sensitive skin, and I nearly come undone.

Desperation pulses inside me, heavy and wanton, my legs turning into jelly. The only reason I don't fall into a puddle at his feet is because of the strong arm wrapped around my waist.

"And I really want to fuck you."

His hand slides beneath my skirt, slow and sure, fingertips brushing my inner thigh, dragging goose-bumps in their wake. When his thumb grazes the soaked fabric of my panties, my hips jerk involuntarily, a moan slipping free.

"I could be wrong," he murmurs, his voice thick with amusement, "but I think you really want me to fuck you, too."

He draws lazy, torturous circles against the wet cotton. It's too much and not nearly enough at the same time. I can't think. Can't speak. All I can do is feel.

"Tell me, Claire," he growls, his breathing becoming ragged as he increases the pressure of his thumb. "Tell me you want me to fuck you."

"I want you to fuck me," I respond without hesitation.

I can't remember ever wanting something as badly as I want this.

Needing something as badly as I need this. As I need Declan.

"Good girl."

Oh. My. *God.*

I didn't realize anything in my life was missing.

Until I heard this sinfully sexy older man call me a good girl.

That's it. My life is now complete.

I can die happy.

But not until I know what an orgasm from him feels like.

His lips crash into mine again, but this time the urgency is different, more possessive, more claiming. I barely notice when his hand leaves me. I'm too caught up in the heat of his mouth, the taste of him, the way he steers me toward the bed like a man on a mission.

I reach for his suit jacket and hastily push it off his shoulders, the sound of fabric hitting the floor like music to my goddamn ears. Then I fumble with the buttons of his shirt, my erratic motions making the task more difficult.

"Impatient?" he muses as he brings our kiss to an end, amusement dancing in his dark blue eyes.

"More like…horny."

"Well, then…" His voice turns molten. "Let's see what we can do about your little…situation."

He steps back a fraction, his gaze locked on mine as he unfastens his shirt one button at a time. There's something deliberate in the way he moves. Controlled, almost reverent.

And when he parts the fabric and shrugs the shirt from his shoulders, I forget how to breathe.

Holy hell.

His chest is broad and sculpted, his abs tight, every muscle defined beneath golden skin. A light dusting of hair trails down his stomach, and tattoos inked in bold lines stretch across his left shoulder and bicep. They appear military in nature. Navy, if I had to guess. There's another marking along his ribs, partially obscured by shadow, but even without reading it, I can tell it means something. Something earned.

He's not what I expected. Not soft. Not slightly out of shape like some older men.

No. Declan is lean, powerful, carved from experience and discipline.

And maybe sin.

"Like what you see?" he asks, that cocky glint flashing in his eyes as he catches me staring.

I lift a brow, pretending to play it cool. "Not bad for an old guy."

He grins, slow and wolfish, then drags me hard against him. His hips roll against mine in a lazy grind that steals my breath.

"Careful, sweetheart. You keep calling me old, and I might have to show you just how young I feel."

"You won't get any complaints from me," I exhale as heat floods my veins.

"Good." He releases me, increasing the distance once more. "Your turn."

"My turn?"

"I stripped for you. Time for you to return the favor."

My stomach flips. The room suddenly feels too warm. Too bright. The golden lamplight spills across the space, casting no shadows, no places to hide.

Just him. Watching. Waiting.

I can't help but feel self-conscious about everything. This man is definitely much more experienced than I am. I've had sex before, but have never been too adventurous. What if I'm not what he wants? What if I take off my clothes and the fantasy fizzles out? What if I disappoint him?

As if able to read my thoughts, Declan's features soften and he steps forward again, cupping my cheek in his large hand. The gesture is tender, at complete odds with the man who was devouring me with his eyes seconds ago.

"If you've changed your mind," he murmurs, brushing his thumb along my cheekbone, "that's okay. I don't want you to feel pressured or forced. I just…" His jaw flexes. "I haven't felt this sort of connection to someone in a long time. I may have gotten a little carried away."

I meet his gaze, the sincerity within almost too much. He's not just saying it to make me feel better. He's saying it because he means it.

It only makes me want him more.

"I haven't changed my mind," I whisper.

Relief flickers behind his eyes, but I press on before doubt can creep back in.

"I just…might need you to take charge. Tell me what to do. That way I don't have to think too much."

He arches a single brow. "Is that what you want? To not have to think?"

I nod. "I can be an overthinker. So right now… Yes. That's what I want. What I need."

He studies me, his gaze unreadable as he steps back and sits on the edge of the bed. My pulse skitters, nerves tangling in my stomach. For a moment, I worry he's about to change his mind.

Then his expression shifts, no longer soft or teasing.

It hardens.

Darkens.

Demands.

"Strip," he orders, his voice thundering through the stillness in the room. "Now."

FIVE

Declan

Silence stretches between us, the air thick and charged, as I wait for her to do as I asked. *Plead* with her to do as I asked.

I've seen my fair share of naked women in my forty-two years.

I've never been so damn desperate to see *this* woman naked.

There's something about her. Something different from any other woman. She strips me bare without touching me. And yet, I'm already unraveling.

Her eyes remain glued to mine as she kicks off her heels one by one before untucking her blouse, her fingers slipping beneath the hem to find the side zipper of her skirt. I don't move. I don't speak. I just watch. Captivated. Aroused. A man brought to his fucking knees by a woman who doesn't even realize the power she holds over me.

Her skirt pools around her ankles, and she steps out of it with an effortless confidence that shouldn't be as erotic as it is. Then her fingers move to the buttons of her blouse. One by one, they pop open, revealing soft, luminous skin with each slow flick.

My fists clench. My cock throbs. She's *killing* me.

I've never wanted someone the way I want her right now. Not just the physical, though that's a storm all of its own. But the way she looks at me. Like she knows me. Like she sees straight through every barrier I've spent years building.

Her blouse slips down her shoulders, baring more of the smooth skin I ache to touch, and she's standing in nothing but her bra and panties. Pale pink. Delicate. Feminine.

Utterly devastating.

My mouth goes dry. I can feel my blood rushing, every inch of me desperate to feel her. Consume her.

Devour her.

"Keep going." My voice is a low rasp, barely audible.

She glances at the pants still covering my lower half. "*You* still have clothes on."

I almost laugh. *Almost.* But I don't let her get away with the distraction.

I slowly rise to my feet, letting every inch of tension between us stretch and tighten. I don't rush, but I don't waste time either. I kick off my shoes, shove down my socks, then grip the waistband of my pants and push them down, briefs and all.

The air hits my skin. So does her heated stare.

Her eyes widen, dark and unreadable as they fix on my hard length.

"Where is that going to fit?" she whispers under her breath.

The corner of my mouth curves. I wrap a hand around my erection and move toward her, close enough to feel the warmth of her body against mine, though we're not touching. Not yet.

"I'll make sure it does," I murmur, low and certain, brushing my mouth against her ear. "And that you enjoy every second of it."

She shivers a full-body tremor, then steps back, her gaze never leaving mine. Reaching behind her, she unclasps her bra. It slips from her shoulders and falls to the floor, revealing the most perfect breasts I've ever seen. Then, with the same aching grace, she hooks her thumbs into the waistband of her panties and pushes them down her legs.

I forget how to fucking breathe.

She's…

Jesus.

Naked. Unashamed. Fucking glorious.

Every inch of her is a goddamn masterpiece. Soft, full curves. Smooth skin begging to be touched.

But it's her eyes that wreck me.

The trust in them. The hunger. The way she looks at me like she *belongs* to me.

"You're so damn beautiful, Claire." My voice cracks with wonder.

But I don't wait for her to respond. I grip the back of her head and crash my mouth against hers.

Her lips part on a gasp as I claim her. The raw, unfiltered sound undoes me. She tastes like mint and wine and something uniquely Claire. Sweet, but with an edge, like the fire she tries to keep hidden.

I dive in deeper, my hands finding her waist, spanning the smooth curve of her hips. Her skin is warm, impossibly soft, and I want to own every inch of it. Memorize her. Brand her into my fucking soul.

Her fingers thread into my hair, gripping tight, and something primal inside me snaps. I deepen the kiss even more, one hand sliding up her ribcage to the underside of her breast. I tease her, circling her taut peak with my thumb until she arches into me, her breath hitching.

"Christ, you feel good," I murmur, dragging my mouth down her jaw, her throat, pausing to worship the delicate dip at the base of it.

I press open-mouthed kisses along her collarbone as my hands roam, learning the shape of her. The swell of her hips. The curve of her lower back. The warmth between her thighs that has me gripping her tighter to keep from losing it entirely.

I want to go slow. Want to make this last. But fuck, I'm barely hanging on.

Her skin flushes beneath my touch, a living canvas reacting to every glide of my fingers, every scrape of my stubble. Her lips are swollen, pupils blown wide with lust, chest rising and falling in quick little bursts.

"You okay?" I ask, my voice rough with restraint.

She nods. "Please don't stop."

She hoists herself onto her toes, her lips brushing against mine, and I'm completely powerless to resist the temptation of her kiss. I guide her backward until her legs bump the edge of the mattress. She sinks onto it, her legs parting for me, welcoming me between them.

I settle over her, and we both freeze for a heartbeat.

Her breath catches.

Mine does, too.

God, she's so warm. So soft. So damn perfect.

I brace one hand beside her head, the other gliding down her side until I reach her thigh.

"I'm going to take my time with you," I murmur against her lips. "You asked me to take control, Claire. And I will. But if there's anything you don't like—"

"I'll tell you," she says, cutting me off with a whisper that feels like a vow.

"Good girl."

I noticed her reaction the last time I said that.

This time, it's even more visceral. Her breath stutters. Her thighs twitch against me. Her eyes flutter shut for a half-second like she's trying to hold herself together… And failing.

I kiss her again, slower this time as I trail my mouth down the line of her jaw. Her neck. Her collarbone.

Her hands thread through my hair, holding on, not guiding, just needing to feel.

I keep inching down her body, pausing at her breasts, my eyes locked on her as I take one perfect peak into my mouth and suck. Slowly. Deeply.

Her back arches, her breathing increasing as her body winds tighter and tighter with every second.

I shift to the other nipple, giving it the same attention, nibbling at the edge of pain. Her whimper splits the air, her body arching even further into me.

"You like that," I murmur, my lips brushing the sensitive skin right above her nipple. "Like the pain."

"Yes," she breathes without hesitation.

"Good girl."

I cover her nipple with my mouth again, biting even harder this time. She gasps, but it turns into a moan. Needy. Desperate. Unhinged.

"You're so damn responsive. I bet your cunt is dripping for me right now. Isn't it?"

"Why don't you find out?" she exhales.

"I plan on it."

I kiss a path down her torso, licking and tasting my way past her navel. She squirms beneath me, her hips pressing upward, but I fight the temptation to rush this.

I said I'd take my time.

I meant it.

I tease her, dragging my tongue along her waist as I run my hand up the inside of her thigh, her muscles clenching when I reach her apex.

But then I retreat.

It's a test in restraint, but I want to savor her. Consume her.

Worship her.

"Please," she whimpers.

"What's that?" I lift my eyes to hers.

"You're killing me."

My mouth curves in the corners. "Trust me. I'll give you what you need." I settle between her legs, pushing her thighs wide. "But you need to be patient."

Hell, *I* need to be patient, too, something that's becoming increasingly difficult, especially as I stare at her dripping pussy that's practically begging for me to bury my face in it.

"Show me what you like."

"What?" Her voice is thick, eyes wide as she props herself on her elbows.

"You heard me." I kiss the inside of her knee. "We only have one night together. I need to make it good for you. So show me what you like." I lean closer to her center. "Show me how you touch yourself. How you get yourself off."

She doesn't do anything for several seconds. Simply stares at me, obviously uncertain about this.

"Get out of your head, Claire. You asked me to take control. Don't think. Just do. I'll never judge you for it."

She draws in a deep breath, then snakes a hand down her stomach, sliding her fingers through her slick folds before finding that bundle of nerves and rubbing.

And I watch.

Watch as she closes her eyes.

Watch as she circles her hips.

Watch as she rubs her clit.

When she glides her fingers lower, sliding one, then another inside her, the restraint I was able to hold on to evaporates. I grab her wrist, stopping her from doing anything further.

"My turn," I growl.

Then I eat her like she's my last meal. Like I've been starved for this. For her.

"Declan…" she moans as I seal my lips around her clit, my fingers thrusting inside her.

"Do you hear that?" I drive in and out of her even faster, the sound of her desire echoing in the room. "Do you hear how wet you are?"

Another moan is the only response I get.

But that's not good enough. I need more.

"Tell me," I demand. "Tell me you hear your wet cunt."

I add another finger, stretching her even more.

"I do."

"And why are you so wet, Claire?" I circle her clit with my tongue, my motions increasing with every second. "Does this delicious pussy need to be fucked?"

"God, yes," she whimpers, her body climbing higher and higher.

"By who? Your friend from the bar earlier?"

"No. By you. I need to be fucked by you," she cries out as an orgasm overtakes her, her legs shaking, body convulsing.

But I don't stop. I continue to thrust into her, savoring the feeling of her walls clenching around my fingers.

Then I crawl up her body, my mouth a whisper from hers.

"Beg for me."

Her eyes fling open, meeting mine. She hesitates, but only for a moment.

"Please fuck me, Declan."

As desperate as I am to slam into her, I need a minute. Otherwise, I'll probably come the second I'm inside her.

"Is that that best you can do? I want you to *really* beg for it, Claire." I tease her opening with my cock. "Tell me everything you want me to do to you. In exact detail."

SIX

Claire

What the hell am I doing?

I don't do things like this. I don't have one-night stands with strangers in hotels. I don't peel back my skin and reveal the raw, unvarnished truth about what I crave, not even to myself.

And I definitely don't give voice to the darkest, dirtiest corners of my desires.

But here I am, perched on the edge of surrender, my heart pounding like a war drum.

I shouldn't want this. Shouldn't want *him*.

He's a stranger I met in a bar, for crying out loud.

And maybe that's precisely *why* I should do this.

He isn't like every other person I've been with — small-town guys who lock up the second I ask for anything beyond basic missionary. Who'd look at me like I've grown horns if I suggest pulling my hair or biting me.

I've spent years pretending I'm content with boring and safe, because anything more makes me feel like I'm asking for too much.

And if I ask for too much, I'm scared I'll chase them away.

But maybe just for tonight, I can give voice to all these things I've kept hidden. I can let myself want. Let myself be greedy. After all, I don't have to worry about chasing Declan away. Not when I'll never see him again.

Taking a breath, I push down the fear and let my desire overpower any feelings of shame.

"I want it rough." The words tumble out before I can stop them. "Want you to stretch me open with that thick cock." Heat spreads across my cheeks, but I keep going. "I want to feel it deep. Feel you everywhere. I want you to use me. Mark me. Spank me. Pull my hair. Make it hurt. And when you don't think I can handle any more, I want you to keep going. I want you to fuck me so hard I'll feel you for weeks."

There. It's out now. Exposed.

And the moment hangs between us like a live wire.

Declan stills, a muscle in his jaw flexing. Something carnal and untamed flickers in his eyes. He inhales like he's trying to keep himself on a leash that's already fraying.

"There's just one problem with that."

Heat rushes over my cheeks as my heart plummets to the pit of my stomach.

Of course. I've scared him off. Gone too far. Confirmed what I've always been afraid of.

"It's okay," I blurt out, averting my gaze. "I didn't mean—"

He cuts me off with a kiss that's anything but gentle. He tastes like lust and desire. And I drink him in.

"I'd love nothing more than to give you every last thing on your wish list."

I blink, brows furrowing. "Then—"

"I don't have a condom." His voice drops. "I wasn't exactly expecting to spend the night fucking a gorgeous, insatiable woman while in town on business."

That piece of information endears me to him a little more. Like I surprised him as much as he's surprised me.

"I'm on birth control. And it's been a while since I've done this sort of thing."

"Same for me. I'll still pull out to be safe, if that's okay."

"Okay," I exhale.

"Okay." He covers my mouth with his, his tongue

tangling with mine in a too-short kiss. When his eyes meet mine once more, they're heated.

Feral.

"Now tell me again to fuck you."

"Declan…" I rake my fingers through his hair and lean into the crook of his neck, nibbling on his earlobe. "I want you to fuck me."

An animalistic growl rips through the room as he straightens, pushing my legs wide and bringing his erection up to me. Then, with one brutal thrust, he's inside me.

I scream. Loud. Unfiltered. My body arches off the bed as he buries himself deep, his cock thick and unforgiving.

"Good girl," he snarls, grinding deeper, his breath hot against my cheek. "Taking every inch of my cock like the needy girl you are."

I don't know how he does it, but he says exactly what I want to hear. What I *need* to hear.

My fingers dig into his shoulders, every nerve ending inside me lighting up. I want more.

I want *everything*.

He grabs my wrists and pins them above my head, locking me in place. Then he fucks me. Not tenderly. Not sweetly.

Ruthlessly. Possessively. Completely.

"Is this what you wanted?" he rasps. "To be used like this? Fucked until you can't think straight?"

"Yes," I moan. "More. Please."

He releases my wrists only to wrap his hand around my throat. Not enough to cut off air. Just enough to let me know he's in control. That I'm his to command. His to ruin.

Then he bites me. Hard. First on the side of my neck, then lower, right above my breast. The pain only sharpens everything. My legs wrap tighter around him.

I need him deeper. Harder. I need to be filled and claimed and completely undone.

When he pulls out, I whimper, ready to beg, but his voice goes dark and rough.

"Hands and knees."

I scramble into position, my legs shaking, mind whirling.

He slams into me from behind, one hand fisting in my hair, yanking my head back as his other hand smacks my ass. The crack echoes through the room. My walls clench in response.

"Say you're mine," he snarls.

"I…" I trail off, struggling to catch my breath.

He spanks me again, and the pain pulls the words from me.

"I'm yours," I gasp. "Fuck. I'm yours."

He growls like a beast unchained and pounds into me harder until I'm shaking with the force of it. I'm dripping. Desperate. Falling apart beneath him.

"You're close, aren't you?"

"So close," I pant.

When he pulls out again, I nearly sob.

"Ask for permission first," he grunts, teasing me with the head of his cock. "Only good girls who ask permission get to come again."

God, he's going to make me say it. I should be embarrassed. Should hate being at someone's mercy. But I've never felt so damn alive.

"Please let me come."

"That's not exactly asking permission, is it?"

"Please, Declan. May I please come?"

He slams into me so hard I cry out. I barely last a few seconds before my orgasm crashes into me like a tidal wave. My entire body convulses, legs shaking uncontrollably as I squeeze around him, clenching and releasing, completely wrecked.

But he's not done.

He pulls out again and flips me onto my back. I blink up at him, dazed and shaking, my breath still coming in shallow bursts.

"Tell me where you want it," he demands, stroking himself over me.

My mind reels as I consider the possibilities.

"Now, Claire." His words are almost a plea as he struggles to hold on to what little control his has left.

I could just tell him my stomach, like every other guy I've been with has done.

But I don't want tonight to be like every other sexual encounter. I want this to stay with me forever. So I give in to my baser desires.

I part my lips, not saying a word. Just open my mouth and stick out my tongue.

His eyes darken. "Fuck." He fists himself harder, his face scrunched almost in pain. The pleasure covering every inch of him is a sight to behold. Unhinged. Unabashed.

Beautiful.

It doesn't take long for hot, thick spurts of cum to explode from his dick, painting my tongue, my cheek, my chin. It's messy and raw and so goddamn perfect.

"Swallow," he orders.

I eagerly obey his command, savoring the salty taste of him.

"Does my good girl want more?"

I nod.

"Open for me."

Again, I follow his command and part my lips.

He leans in and swipes my cheek, collecting every drop. He presses his fingers between my lips, and I suck them clean, never breaking eye contact.

"Good fucking girl," he groans.

I swallow everything, my body still trembling, my brain a haze of endorphins and aftershocks.

"I'd get a towel," he murmurs, "but I want you to sleep with my cum on your face tonight."

I try to smile, but it's shaky. Before I can stop it, that old, ugly feeling creeps back in. The shame. The part of me that thinks there must be something wrong with me for wanting these things.

I drop my gaze, suddenly very aware of my nakedness. Of how I must look to him. Of what he must think of me now.

But he notices. Of course he does.

He tilts my chin up, gentle but firm.

"Hey." His voice is softer now. Tender. "Don't do that."

"Do what?" I try to laugh, but it comes out brittle.

He brushes his knuckles along my cheek. "Act like you should be ashamed of what you like." His eyes hold mine, and I can't look away. "There's nothing wrong with what we just did, Claire. *Nothing*. It's normal to want this. Exploring what turns you on doesn't make you depraved or broken or whatever's going through your head right now. It makes you *honest*. Real. I'd rather be with someone like that than someone who tells me what she thinks I want to hear."

Tears burn behind my eyes, and I fight to blink them back.

This man is a complete stranger, yet he sees me more clearly than any other man in my life ever has.

"And if I didn't need to get on a plane back home tomorrow morning," he continues, dragging his gaze down my body with quiet reverence, "I'd spend a lot more time helping you figure out what else you like."

A small smile finds its way to my lips. I've never been with anyone like him before. Maybe that's been my problem. Maybe I need an older man, one who's experienced enough to know how to please a woman.

And Declan most definitely knows how to please me.

"Well," I murmur, dragging my fingers through his disheveled dark hair. "My flight doesn't leave for another ten hours."

His brow arches. "Oh yeah?"

I give a few slow nods. "Yeah."

"And how would you like to spend those ten hours?" He inches his lips toward mine.

I hook a leg around his waist and roll him onto his back, grinning as I feel him start to harden against me again.

"I have a few ideas."

SEVEN

Declan

The first thing I notice is the light.

Pale gold filters in through the gap in the curtains, brushing over the bed in soft stripes. It touches Claire's cheekbone, the curve of her hips, the delicate skin of her shoulders where I pressed my mouth hours ago.

She's still asleep, her hair a wild, sexy mess, the duvet pulled low, baring the long, graceful line of her spine. One arm is curled beneath the pillow, the other draped along her body.

She looks like a goddamn dream. Better than a dream. Because dreams fade. But last night? Last night is permanently burned into me.

I've woken up next to women before. Had flings.

Nights that meant nothing. That were an escape. A way to shut off my mind for a few hours.

But this doesn't feel like nothing.

It never did.

I let my gaze drift over her, memorizing every detail. The small bruises blooming on her hips where I held her too tightly. The faint red marks on her ass. The indentation of my teeth on her neck. All proof of how ravenous we were for each other. How unrestrained we were.

How damn *perfect* we were.

But it's not just the roughness that's completely unraveled me.

It's the way her body kept finding mine in the dark.

Like when I woke to her climbing on top of me. No words. No desperate pleas. Just heat and need.

Her hair had spilled forward as she sank down onto me, slow and deliberate. Her hips moved in these slow, mesmerizing circles. Like she wanted to draw out every second. Every motion. Every damn heartbeat.

She'd tilted her head back, her lips parted, eyes fluttering closed as she savored the way we fit.

I'd gripped her waist, not to control her, but to steady myself. To *savor* her.

She wasn't rushing. Wasn't trying to perform. She

just *was.* Riding the edge of something deeper than just pleasure. Something that felt almost sacred.

She leaned forward, bracing her hands on my chest, and whispered my name in the softest, breathiest voice. Not begging. Not demanding. Just saying it. Like it meant something.

Like *I* meant something.

In that moment, I wanted to mean something. Wanted to mean *everything*, even if I have no right to want that.

This wasn't supposed to be anything. Just one night. A reprieve. A distraction from the news I received yesterday.

But Claire isn't a distraction. She's something else entirely.

Something far more dangerous.

I drag a hand down my face and glance at the clock on the nightstand, cursing under my breath when I see the time. 7:15.

My flight leaves in a few hours, and after yesterday's storm and all the cancellations, the airport's going to be chaos. I can't afford to miss it. I have oral arguments to prepare for. Briefs to write. A life to return to.

I quietly slip out of bed, careful not to wake Claire. My body aches in the best kind of way, spent but deeply satisfied.

I dress one piece at a time, taking longer than necessary, if only to delay the inevitable.

But when I'm fully clothed, I have no choice. I need to go.

I drink her in one last time. She looks so peaceful, her lips curved faintly in the kind of smile that makes me wonder what she's dreaming about. As much as I want to wake her to say goodbye, I don't want to steal that from her. Not when she gave me more over the past several hours than I had any right to ask for.

Instead, I cross the room and find the hotel notepad on the desk. My handwriting's a little rough but legible as I scratch out a quick note.

Claire,

Last night was unexpected. And unforgettable. One of the best nights I've had in a long time.

All my best,

Declan

I tap the pen against the paper, hesitating. Then I add one last line below my name.

Here's my number. Maybe our paths will cross again. I hope they do.

After adding my cell number, I fold the note and place it on the pillow beside her, where my head rested just a few minutes ago.

I linger longer than I should, my fingers grazing the edge of the sheet. I want to crawl back in beside her. Pull her into my chest. Bury my face in her neck and breathe her in.

But I can't.

I may not know her well, but I know enough that she doesn't need someone like me in her life. She deserves someone better. Someone who can open his heart to her. That's not me.

With that reminder, I turn and walk out the door.

EIGHT

Claire

I inhale a deep breath, savoring the comforting aroma of pine and fresh earth. The cold nips at my cheeks and seeps through the seams of my coat, but I don't mind. There's a kind of magic in the crispness of the December air that's always invigorated me.

Across the lawn, the Holley Ridge Christmas tree towers above everything, a giant Norway spruce that's become the center of the annual Christmas festival. With the tree-lighting ceremony mere days away, the Sycamore Falls Fire Department is currently hard at work decorating it with thousands of twinkling lights.

I'm not the only one watching them, either.

It seems like every single female within a fifty-mile

radius has decided to stop by Holley Ridge today for coffee or hot chocolate. Instead of cozying up by the fireplace inside the beautiful lobby, they've opted for seats on the large wraparound porch where the view of the tree and the firefighters is unobstructed.

"It's definitely the most wonderful time of the year," a familiar voice croons.

I smile as Grandma Estelle sidles up beside me, her cherry-red coat buttoned to the neck, a matching shade painted boldly across her lips. Her eyes, however, are fixed on the tree. Or more accurately, the broad-shouldered firefighter in dark blue pants and a thermal Henley whose muscles flex with every movement.

There was a time I found firefighters universally hot, apart from my future brother-in-law, Finn. Sure, he's attractive, but he's always been my sister's best friend, so I never really saw him that way. Not like I did the other guys in the department.

But now?

I feel nothing. Not even a flutter. Not even for Murphy, who looks like he stepped off the cover of a firefighter charity calendar — perfect smile, dark hair, strong physique.

Because no matter who I look at, I find myself comparing them to Declan.

I try not to. God knows I've tried. But nothing has been the same since Boston. Since *him.*

I haven't told a soul about the night I allowed myself to give in to my desires. I thought about telling my sister. Or my best friend and roommate, Dylan.

In the end, I decided it didn't matter.

Or maybe I didn't *want* it to matter.

But the truth is, that one night has left a mark I can't scrub clean.

I still have the note Declan left, tucked away in the back of my desk drawer like a secret I can't let go of. I've certainly read that note more times than I care to admit.

But I never texted.

Never called.

I'm not sure what's stopped me. Maybe I'm scared the magic won't be there. That it won't be like I remember.

Or maybe I'm scared he'll have changed his mind now that the fog of our incredible night together has faded.

I'm not sure I can handle that sort of rejection.

"I hope you enjoy the show today, Grandma Estelle," I say with a smile.

"You know I will." She gives me a waggle of her brow before returning her attention to the firefighters, pulling out a pair of binoculars from her purse with zero shame.

I simply shake my head and laugh as I continue walking through the grounds.

Contractors and volunteers bustle around like elves, erecting rows of stalls for the Christmas festival where locals will sell handmade ornaments, sugar cookies, and piping hot cider. The North Pole cabin is nearly ready for Santa's arrival, and the ice-skating rink already gleams beneath strings of lights.

In just a few days, this place will be a winter wonderland.

And I need everything to be perfect.

"Claire!" Parker's voice cuts through as I snap photos with my phone to use in social media posts promoting the upcoming festival. My boss approaches, her cheeks pink from the cold, her smile bright. "This place looks amazing. Seriously. You've outdone yourself."

A warmth blooms inside of me. "I learned from the best."

I grew up coming to Holley Ridge every year with my mom and sister, watching in awe as Parker's dad transformed the ranch into something straight out of a snow globe. After he passed, Parker made it even bigger to honor his memory.

Now I get to be a part of it, too.

It means a great deal that she's put her trust in me to continue the tradition her parents started, and I want nothing more than to prove myself.

"Don't sell yourself short, Claire. I've seen the ticket numbers. Not to mention, this place is booked solid from now until after the new year. I wasn't sure that would happen with all the new rooms we've added during the renovation. But thanks to the marketing and influencer outreach you've done, this is shaping up to be the biggest year ever for Holley Ridge." A hint of nostalgia twinkles in her eyes. "Dad would love to know his love for Christmas is now being shared with all these people. Thanks for that. For being part of this family."

An unexpected wave of emotion washes over me. "Thank you for this opportunity."

Before Parker can say anything else, I spot Joshua walking toward me, his stride purposeful, his face a little more serious than usual.

"Hey," he says, tucking his hands into the pockets of his fleece-lined jacket. A few tufts of dark hair sprout out of his beanie, and some scruff dots his jawline.

Joshua is nothing like Declan, but the dark hair and scruff reminds me of him.

Then again, everything seems to remind me of him these days.

"Got a second?"

I hesitate, glancing toward Parker to make sure she doesn't need me for anything else.

"I'll talk to you later," she says, obviously sensing whatever Joshua needs isn't work-related. "I should go make sure Grandma Estelle doesn't turn into an ice cube from spending all day in the cold ogling those firefighters."

"It *is* the most wonderful time of the year, as she says," I reply with a laugh.

"She's not the only one who thinks so." She gestures at the dozens of women sitting on the back porch.

"Gotta love small towns."

"I wouldn't want to live anywhere else," Parker sings as she heads toward the towering Norway spruce, leaving me alone with Joshua.

At one point, I may have felt a bit awkward being around him like this, considering our history. But we worked through it. Realized we were always better off as friends than romantic partners.

Now I can't imagine not having him as a friend.

"Is everything okay?" I ask, noticing his nervous expression.

He glances around, as if he wants to be sure we won't be overheard. "Do you remember that ancestry kit we did a while back?"

"Of course. You were so excited when you learned you were Scottish. Started saving money to go one day."

"I still am." He gives a soft laugh, but it fades quickly. "I made my results public a few months ago. Just on a whim, I guess. Since I don't know much about my father, apart from my mom telling me he was a guy she had a one-night stand with back in college, I thought maybe I'd match with a distant cousin or something."

"Did you?" I ask, all too familiar with his desire to learn more about his family, particularly after losing his mother to cancer early this year.

"I did. Only it wasn't a cousin." He pauses, drawing in a small breath. "It was my father."

"Are you serious?" My eyes widen. "Did you reach out?"

He nods. "Honestly, I didn't expect a response. If I were in his shoes and a random person messaged me after an ancestry kit claimed we had a close familial DNA match indicating he could be my father, I'm not sure I would have answered. But he did. We messaged back and forth, and he said he remembered my mother, but never knew she was pregnant. He was in San Diego on shore leave from the navy, had a few drinks at a bar, and one thing led to another…"

"Wow. That's… That's incredible." I wrap my arms around Joshua. "I'm so happy for you."

This time last year, I never would have been able to hug him like this. Not after he'd proposed. But it was obvious he only did so out of grief due to his mother's decision to enter hospice. For a brief moment, I nearly agreed, scared to lose him as a friend.

Now we're back to being the friends we were

before we overcomplicated things. Hell, these days, he's more than just a friend. He's family. Someone I can't imagine my life without.

"Thanks, Claire." He pulls back, shifting his weight from foot to foot. "He's in San Francisco for business next week and has agreed to meet up for dinner before heading home. I was sort of hoping you'd come with me."

"Me?"

"I just thought it'd be nice to have someone there with me. Plus, you're so good with people. You always know what to say. Having you there might help with my nerves."

Of course he'd ask me. Joshua and I have always understood each other in ways most people don't. We both grew up without fathers. The difference is I knew mine chose to walk away, while Joshua never even had a name.

I give him a reassuring smile. "I'll be there."

Relief washes over his expression. "Thanks. It means a lot."

He wraps me in a hug, and I hold him tightly before pulling back with a smile. "Now go salt the walkways before someone breaks a leg."

He mock salutes. "Yes, ma'am." Then he walks off in the direction of the large garage on the edge of the property that's essentially his home base as the head groundskeeper of Holley Ridge.

I get back to work, shooting videos and photos of all the behind-the-scenes stuff going on to make this year's Christmas festival the best yet. I'm not too proud to admit I capture several minutes of the firefighters working on the Christmas tree. They're social media gold.

"That boy is lucky to have you," Grandma Estelle calls out as I zoom in on a few of the firefighters.

I grin, shifting my gaze to meet hers. "I'm lucky to have him, too."

We may have made more than our fair share of mistakes when we were younger. But we grew out of them. Learned from them. What's left is something stronger. Steadier.

I wouldn't trade my friendship with Joshua for anything in the world.

NINE

Claire

I'm already ten minutes late, and I still have to finish applying my makeup.

I jab the mascara wand back into the tube with a muttered curse, rummaging one-handed through my jewelry box until I find the dainty hoops I planned to wear.

This is the absolute worst time to go to dinner with Joshua, considering the tree-lighting ceremony is tomorrow night, which is the official kick-off of the Holley Ridge Christmas Festival. My to-do list is longer than Santa's infamous list, and I haven't checked off a single thing today that didn't feel like a minor emergency.

But he needs me. He'd never let me go through

something like this alone. I can't let him either, even if it means pulling an all-nighter editing videos and graphics for this week's launch.

My phone buzzes against the vanity as I apply my lipstick. I don't have to look to know it's Joshua. I tap on the message and read his text.

JOSHUA:

Just making sure you're okay.

I've known him long enough to understand it's his nice way of asking where the hell I am.

But Joshua would never come right out and say something like that. He's always been exceedingly polite. He would never pull my hair or bite me during sex. Not like Declan did.

The memory flashes sharp and hot through me, leaving a trail of heat in its wake, my core aching with need.

I squeeze my eyes shut, telling myself to stop thinking about him. The last thing I need right now is a distraction. And that's all thinking about Declan would be.

I type out a quick reply to Joshua.

ME:

About to head out the door. I'll be there in fifteen minutes.

I toss my phone into my purse and finish lining my eyes.

In retrospect, I probably shouldn't have come home, considering I didn't leave Holley Ridge until thirty minutes before our dinner reservation, which is *at* Holley Ridge.

But I couldn't show up looking like I'd just crawled out of a tinsel explosion. I needed a shower. Time to rinse off the day and breathe.

When I pull into the staff lot behind Holley Ridge fifteen minutes later, the inn glows like a Christmas card come to life. Twinkling lights strung across every eave and arch. Evergreen garlands draped with ribbons and snow-dusted pinecones. Wreaths hung from every window.

As I make my way toward the main entrance, a couple walks past, smiling and laughing, their cheeks flushed, breath visible in the chilly air. Another couple takes a selfie in front of the life-size nutcracker. I'm about to remind them to tag Holley Ridge in any social media posts, but stop myself. I'm already running late.

I hurry through the front doors, waving at Heidi as I pass the check-in desk and follow the garland-lined hallway toward the restaurant overlooking the lake. The thousands of lights throughout the property dance across the water, their glow making the snow shimmer.

"Hey, Claire," Moira says from behind the hostess stand when she sees me. "Joshua's already here." She leans closer, lowering her voice. "And now I see where he gets those good looks from. His dad is *fine*. Like, silver fox in a Tom Ford ad fine."

"That's nice, I guess." I give her a tight smile, unsure how I'm supposed to respond.

"They're by the windows," she says cheerily.

"Thanks," I murmur, then weave through the restaurant, smiling at various members of the wait-staff as I go, my heels clicking against the polished wood floor.

Joshua's eyes find mine the second I turn the corner, his expression lighting up as he stands to greet me.

"Thanks for being here." He brushes a soft kiss to my cheek, wrapping me in a quick hug.

"Sorry I'm late."

"It's okay. You have a lot going on right now. I appreciate you taking the time."

He helps me out of my coat, then rests his hand on the small of my back, steering me toward the table where a well-dressed man in a suit faces the windows.

"Claire," Joshua begins, "I'd like you to meet my father."

The man stands and turns toward me.

First, I take in the outline of his jaw. Sharp.

Square. Shadowed with the perfect amount of stubble.

Then the slope of his nose. The curve of his mouth.

When his eyes meet mine, I inhale a sharp breath, feeling like the world is about to give out beneath me.

I know those eyes. Blue. Bright. Unmistakable.

I've seen them up close, glazed with heat, dark with hunger.

I've felt the weight of that gaze on my skin. Dreamt of it, then forced myself to forget.

Convinced myself it was for the best. That we lived in two different worlds. That our paths would never cross again.

He goes completely still, his expression flatlining in a single frozen beat of recognition that mirrors my own.

We stare at each other, the room around us falling into silence like someone's hit mute on the world.

No ambient music. No clinking glass. No polite conversation.

Just the sound of my own heartbeat roaring in my ears.

I try to speak, to say something, but my mouth won't cooperate.

Joshua's voice cuts through the fog, cheerful and proud. "Declan, this is my good friend, Claire Thomas. Claire, this is my father… Declan Hart."

Father.

The word lands like a blow. It rings in my ears. Lodges in my throat.

Declan's gaze never leaves mine as we're both forced to come to terms with this truth.

My one-night stand, the man I can't stop thinking about, is the father of the man I gave my virginity to.

TEN

Declan

For a moment, I forget how to breathe.

It feels like all the air's been sucked out of the room, the lights overhead too bright. My pulse stutters in my ears, drowning out Joshua's voice.

I've imagined Claire a hundred different ways since I left Boston. Her body draped over mine. Her laughter echoing around me. Her hair tangled in my hands. I've replayed that night like a favorite song, one I knew I'd never hear again but couldn't stop humming anyway.

For the past few weeks, every time my phone buzzed, I jumped for it, hopeful it was her.

It never was.

I was so desperate I even resorted to trying to find her on social media. Turns out "Claire from California" doesn't exactly narrow the playing field. I didn't know her last name. Didn't know what she did. Didn't even know if she was real or some illusion conjured by scotch and regret.

I thought it was a lost cause. Thought I'd go the rest of my life without seeing Claire again.

I never imagined I'd see her here. With my son.

I blink, making sure I'm not imagining her. That this isn't simply a manifestation of my deepest desires.

It's not.

No matter how hard I try to blink it away, she's still here.

And she looks even more beautiful than I remember. Her dark hair falls in waves over her shoulders, a simple black dress clinging to her curves in a way that should be illegal. But what has my attention, much like in Boston, are her lips. Painted red. Full. Plump.

And what makes it even worse is that I know how those lips feel. How they move. How they taste.

What I wouldn't give to have one more taste.

But that ship has sailed. Especially now.

I force my expression into something neutral. Calm. In complete control when I'm anything but.

"It's nice to meet you, Claire." I extend my hand toward her.

The seconds seem to stretch as she eyes me, like

she's still processing this turn of events, too. After what feels like an eternity, she finally places her hand in mine.

The instant our skin touches, the same sensation of warmth and fire I experienced during our one night returns. But it's even more electric. Even more thrilling.

"You, too," she replies in that same soft voice I've imagined moaning my name more times than I care to admit.

I reluctantly let go, reaching to pull out her chair, but Joshua is already there, helping her sit.

As I lower myself into my own chair, I glance between Joshua and Claire, trying to figure out their relationship. When Joshua said he'd invited a friend to join us, I imagined another guy. Not a woman.

Not the woman who I had begging me to fuck her mere weeks ago.

"I ordered you a glass of sparkling rosé to start, since I know you like to pair your drink with your meal," Joshua says to Claire, gesturing to the bubbling champagne glass in front of her.

"Thanks," she replies with a tight smile.

I may not know her well, but I can physically feel the nervous energy radiating off her.

I've been to my fair share of uncomfortable dinners. But this one may just take the cake.

"The filet here is great," Joshua offers, opening his

menu, completely oblivious to the tension simmering between Claire and me.

"I'll keep that in mind," I reply, taking a sip of my scotch and stealing a brief glance at Claire.

She's not the carefree, flirty woman I met in Boston. The woman who laughed with abandon. Who leaned into my touch like she needed it.

This woman is tightly wound. Guarded. Less spark, more steel.

And yet, she still makes my pulse race.

"Are you going to get the salmon?" Joshua asks her.

She jumps, darting her eyes toward him. "What did you say?"

He studies her warily. "Are you okay?"

There's something intimate about the way he curves toward her, making me think they were once more than just friends.

The idea sends sparks of jealousy through me.

"Of course," she replies in a voice pitched too high.

At least, higher than I remember.

She briefly closes her eyes, taking a calming breath. When she opens them again, they find mine, and she quickly pushes back from the table.

"If you'll just excuse me for a minute." She looks at Joshua. "Nature calls." She rises to her feet.

I do, as well, the gentleman in me reacting on instinct.

"If our server comes back, order me the salmon and a glass of chardonnay," she instructs Joshua.

"You got it."

Her eyes briefly meet mine before she hurries away from the table. If she moved any faster, she'd be running.

"Sorry if she seems a little on edge," Joshua explains as I return to my seat. "She's been working constantly lately."

I nod, doing everything to keep my attention on Joshua and not steal a glance at Claire's retreating frame.

Especially the ass I remember spanking.

"What does she do?" I ask.

"She's the head of marketing for the resort." He leans back in his chair, pride warming his tone. "She's basically been organizing the entire Holley Ridge Christmas Festival, which is a huge annual event around here. The tree-lighting ceremony is tomorrow night. She's been going nonstop for weeks."

So she's in charge of Christmas.

Of course she is. It suits her. At least what I learned of her during our night together.

"I saw the lights on the drive in. It's stunning."

He smiles. "That's all her. Claire's determined. In

the best way. When she wants something, she goes after it with everything she has. That's what she's been doing since the owner of this place hired her. Proving she has what it takes to do this job, despite her age."

"How old is she?" I ask hesitantly.

"Same as me. Twenty-four."

I nod, grateful for that. At least she's not younger.

"You work here, too. Correct?" I sip my scotch.

"Yeah. I do a bit of everything. My official title is head groundskeeper. I've worked here since I turned sixteen and have done pretty much every job there is, from bussing tables at this restaurant to maintenance to everything in between."

"Sounds like you've made yourself pretty indispensable."

"I'd like to think so."

A brief silence passes between us. I should use this opportunity to learn more about him, but I can't stop thinking about Claire and who she is to Joshua.

"So, you and Claire," I say after a beat. "Are you two just friends, or is there something more?"

I feel myself hold my breath as I wait for his response, fearful I've already fucked up whatever relationship I might have with Joshua before we've had a chance to get to know each other.

"There used to be." He shrugs, lifting his beer.

"Used to be?" I prod, needing more of the story.

Not because I'm interested in learning about my son, which is the only reason I should be questioning him about this.

But because I want to know more about Claire.

"We realized we were better off as friends. And we are."

I nod, unsure if I should be relieved over the idea that he no longer has any romantic feelings for her, or horrified over the possibility that my son and I may have slept with the same woman.

Claire returns a moment later, and I feel her before I see her. Just like in Boston. She sits back down, her movements careful. Thankfully, the waiter shows up then, giving me a brief reprieve from my unnerving thoughts as we place our dinner order.

Once we're alone again, Joshua turns the conversation toward Claire, bragging about her accomplishments like the proud friend he clearly is. She smiles through it, but it's strained.

"This dinner's supposed to be about you two. Not me," she says after several minutes of Joshua regaling me with all the hard work she's put in over the past several months. It's obvious she doesn't take compliments well. "What do you do, Declan?"

She turns to me, but doesn't look me directly in the eyes, everything about her stiff and tense, a complete opposite from the carefree and relaxed woman I was lucky enough to spend one incredible night with.

"I'm a lawyer."

"In D.C., correct?"

"How did you know that?" Joshua asks, furrowing his brow.

Claire hesitates, her lips parting as she struggles to come up with an explanation. "You must have mentioned it," she finally says with a soft smile.

He studies her for a beat, and I'm convinced he can sense something is off. If they're as close as they seem to be, it wouldn't be too hard for him to realize she's not being completely truthful.

"I'm so sorry to disturb you, Joshua," an older woman interjects as she approaches our table, pulling his attention away from Claire. "There's a problem with several of the heaters on the south lawn. I hate to ask, but do you mind taking a look at them?"

"Of course." He pushes to his feet, looking between Claire and me. "This shouldn't take long."

"Certainly," I respond, although I can sense Claire's nerves over the prospect of being left alone with me. She doesn't show it, though.

"We'll be fine," she assures him.

He gives her a small smile, then follows the petite woman, leaving me alone with Claire for the first time since Boston.

Earlier this morning, I didn't think I'd ever hear from her again, let alone *see* her.

And now we're sitting mere inches away from each other in a darkened restaurant overlooking an idyllic lake.

Claire purposefully avoids looking at me, directing her attention out the windows as she fidgets with her hands. The hum of the restaurant fills the awkward silence — clinking silverware, soft holiday music, the murmur of nearby conversations.

I hate everything about it.

When I can't take the tension anymore, I murmur, "Claire."

"Declan," she says at the same time.

We both laugh nervously. God, that laugh. I didn't realize how much I needed to hear it until now.

I gesture toward her with a smile. "Go ahead."

She lifts her chin, a hint of the Claire I saw in Boston returning. "I didn't know who you were that night. If I had…" She trails off, exhaling hard. "It never would've happened."

"I didn't know who you were, either," I respond, then chuckle under my breath. "In fact, the reason I was even in that bar is because I'd just found out about Joshua and I needed something to help me take my mind off the fact that I had a son I never knew about."

"And that was me."

"That was you." I meet her gaze, low and even. "I'm glad it was you. That night… I haven't been able to stop thinking about you."

A blush blooms on her cheeks, and she bites her lower lip to reel in her smile. God, what I wouldn't give to bite that lip like I did in Boston.

But this isn't like Boston.

I know who she is now.

She's my son's friend.

A woman he very well could have slept with.

Who he once had romantic feelings for.

There are some lines even I won't cross.

And this is one of them.

So instead of allowing myself to be drawn into her, I clear my throat and drag my eyes back to my drink.

"Regardless of how incredible that night was or how I haven't been able to stop thinking about you, it's probably for the best if we don't tell him."

She straightens, blinking repeatedly before averting her gaze. "Right. Of course."

"I want to try to build something with him," I explain. "I don't want to risk that by him finding out about us."

Claire is quiet for a long beat, her expression completely unreadable. Finally, she looks my way and forces a smile.

"As far as I'm concerned, there's nothing for him

to find out. It was just one night. We can pretend it never happened."

"Exactly." I swallow hard, hearing those words leave her mouth harder than I thought it would be. "We'll just pretend it never happened."

Although, I get a feeling that's easier said than done.

ELEVEN

Claire

I should be double-checking that the hospitality suite for all the influencers scheduled to arrive today is fully stocked. Or preparing their welcome baskets. Or going over the schedule for tonight's tree-lighting ceremony.

Instead, I'm at my desk, staring out the frosted window and trying not to spiral over last night's revelation.

Declan is Joshua's father.

And I slept with him.

Hell, I did more than sleep with him. I let him see the parts of me I usually keep locked up tight. I let him bite me. Spank me. Use me. Told him my deepest fantasies.

For one glorious night, he fulfilled each and every one of them.

I've often imagined running into him again. Played out different scenarios in my head. What I'd say. What *he'd* say. Whether he'd still look at me with the same heat in his gaze.

Now I know he would.

But I never expected it to be like this.

Never expected for him to be Joshua's father.

The door creaks open, pulling me out of the same circular thoughts I've been stuck in since last night. Genevieve steps inside carrying a long silver bag I can tell holds a bottle of wine. Her growing belly protrudes beneath her wool coat, and she has a permanent glow that has nothing to do with the chilly temperatures outside.

"Oh, you're here," she says, surprised to see me in my office. "I figured you'd be running around like crazy to get things ready for tonight. I just wanted to leave this for you."

She sets the bag on my desk.

"Thanks, Gen. I was just checking my email before the day got away from me," I tell her with a forced smile.

I have pages of last-minute checks I want to do before the thousands of people we're expecting arrive tonight. But my thoughts keep floating back to

Declan. To the moment he stood from the table and the world dropped out from under me.

"Are you okay?" She narrows her gaze on me, scrutinizing my appearance.

I should have known she'd pick up on my unease. She *is* my sister. She knows me better than anyone. Since we were kids, we've shared everything with each other. First crush. First kiss. First time having sex.

The only thing I haven't shared with her is my first one-night stand. I didn't think it mattered. Didn't think it would have any impact on my life other than being a night of incredible sex.

How wrong I was.

"I'm just a little anxious about tonight. I need everything to be perfect."

She pinches her lips together, her analytical gaze continuing to sweep over me. "No, that's not it. Something else is bothering you."

I could just brush it off. Tell her I'm tired from all the hours I've been working. It's not a complete lie.

But it's not the late nights and running on caffeine that's left me exhausted. It's the secret I've been keeping from her. The one that's grown much heavier since last night.

"I had a one-night stand when I was in Boston," I blurt out before I can stop myself.

Her eyes light up, lips curving into a slow grin as

she lowers herself into the chair across from me, resting her hand on her stomach.

"Mom was right after all."

"Maybe," I groan.

After I got back from Boston, Mom claimed she sensed a change in me. Said I gave off an aura of someone who'd been on a journey of sexual enlightenment.

I denied it, saying she was probably mistaking my sister's "aura" for mine.

But she wasn't wrong. My night with Declan was more than just a sexual awakening. It was an experience that's etched itself into my soul, making me wonder if I'll ever find anyone who can make me feel the things he did.

Which makes the truth of who he is even more painful to swallow.

"Who was it?" Genevieve presses. "Someone from the conference?"

"Not exactly." I pause, picking at a loose thread on my cardigan. "Just someone stranded at the same hotel because of the snowstorm. We met at the bar. He was older. Gorgeous. Confident." I can't stop the smile from pulling on my lips. "Flirtatious. So damn sexy. Like he stepped straight out of a romance book."

"Damn." She fans herself. "Sounds intense."

"It was. We stayed at the bar for hours and talked

about everything that popped into our heads. Or, *I* talked. He just listened. Seemed genuinely interested in what I had to say. It was…refreshing. Regardless, I had no intention of it becoming more than just an enjoyable conversation."

"But?" she prods.

"But when he walked me back to my room to make sure I made it safely, I knew I'd regret it if I let him walk away. So I didn't. Then I spent the next several hours having the best sex of my life."

"That good?"

I nod. "If sex were a sport, that man would win a gold medal in each and every event. And there were quite a few events, if you know what I mean."

"Damn." Genevieve fans herself again, giggling.

I love seeing her like this. So carefree. So…happy.

It's so different from how she was this time last year. Recently divorced. Determined to avoid anything remotely resembling romance. Instead, she decided to focus solely on the one thing she *did* want.

A baby.

She probably never expected her best friend, Finn, to be the one to give it to her. I knew it was only a matter of time before she finally realized what's been in front of her all her life.

"So what happened after?" she presses.

"He had an early flight the next morning. When I

woke up, he was gone. At first, I wondered if I imagined it. But then…"

"Yes?"

"I found the note he left."

"What did it say?" she asks, practically bouncing on her seat.

I open the drawer and retrieve the note, handing it to her.

She flashes me a grin before focusing on the paper. "'Dear, Claire. Last night was unexpected. And unforgettable. One of the best nights I've had in a long time. All my best, Declan. Here's my number. Maybe our paths will cross again. I hope they do.'" She lifts her excited eyes to mine. "Did you call him?"

"I thought about it."

"What's stopping you?" She sets the letter on my desk and I put it back in the drawer. "Because he's older? Or because you think you need to spend every waking hour of your life working? Because I—"

"At first, yes to both of those things," I admit.

"At first?"

I slowly nod.

"So you *did* call?"

"I didn't have to. I ran into him again. Last night, actually."

"Where?"

"Here. At the restaurant."

She furrows her brow. "I thought you were having dinner with Joshua and his dad."

"I did." I give her a knowing look.

"And he was there, too?"

I laugh under my breath. "You could say that."

She tilts her head, confusion knitting her brow. "What do you mean?"

I inhale deeply, running my hands down my blouse, steeling myself for what I'm about to admit.

"My one-night stand *is* Joshua's father."

My confession hangs in the air between us as the room falls eerily silent. No polite conversations wafting into my office from the lobby. No music playing in the background. No phone ringing.

It's just me and the truth I'm still struggling to come to terms with.

"You're kidding," Genevieve says, her eyes wide in shock.

"I wish I were."

"So last night, when you showed up at the restaurant to have dinner with Joshua and the dad he just found out about..."

"Yup," I say, nodding miserably. "That was him. Declan. My one-night stand."

She stares, stunned into silence for a full ten seconds, her mouth agape. Then she slumps back into her chair. "Holy shit, Claire. That's...that's some plot twist."

"It wasn't just a plot twist. It was a plot catastrophe. The whole situation was just…" I shake my head, looking for the right word. But there's only one. "It was awful, Gen. Truly awful."

She reaches across the desk and covers my hand with hers, squeezing. "I'm sorry. I can't even imagine what a shock that must have been. Did you two get a chance to talk about it? Clear the air?"

"We did."

"And?"

"We agreed Joshua can't know. Declan just found out he has a son. He wants to be in his life. I refuse to interfere with that."

"For what it's worth, he sounds like a good person," Genevieve offers in consolation. "Like he's taking his new role as a father seriously."

I'm not sure it helps. Because the fact he's a good person makes the truth sting even more.

While I didn't learn much about him during our one night together, apart from the fact that he turned me into a quivering bundle of nerves with one touch, he shared quite a bit about himself last night. And everything I learned solidified what I sensed before inviting him into my hotel room. That he's a decent person.

He served ten years in the navy. Then put himself through college and law school. After graduating, he was recruited by one of the most prestigious civil rights firms in the country. Now he spends his days fighting for the rights of those unable to do so themselves. He's spearheaded some of the top cases in recent history, sometimes taking it all the way up to the Supreme Court. He spoke about his work like it's sacred. Like every client matters. I could have listened to him talk for hours just to be around that passion again.

"So what are you going to do?" Genevieve's voice cuts through, and I snap my gaze back to her.

"Nothing." I shrug. "Joshua has looked for answers about his dad for years. He has those now. And has a dad who wants a relationship." I force a smile. "After everything he's been through over the past several years with his mom, he deserves to have something good in his life. I won't come between that."

"And you think you can be around his father and pretend you never slept together? That it never happened?" I can hear the skepticism in her voice.

"It was one night. It didn't mean anything," I insist, although the words taste sour on my tongue.

My one night with Declan meant more than any other night I've spent with another man in recent history.

Or ever.

"Plus, he's already on his way back to D.C. I doubt I'll see him anytime soon. I was only there last night because Joshua wanted me as a buffer, more or less. Any contact we may have in the future will be minimal at best."

Genevieve gives me a sympathetic smile. "Look on the bright side."

"What's that?"

"You finally broke your dry spell and had some incredible sex."

I sigh, grateful to have a sister who can make light of a serious situation when I need it the most. "Did I ever."

I just wish it wasn't with my ex's father.

TWELVE

Declan

I shouldn't be here.

The thought follows me with every step up the path toward Holley Ridge, my shoes crunching against the dusting of snow.

I should be 38,000 feet in the air on my way back to D.C. That was the plan. Wake up. Pack. Head to the airport. Fly home.

Then Joshua asked if I had time for breakfast before I headed out.

I didn't.

But I also didn't want him to think I was brushing him off. Not after missing the past twenty-four years. So I said yes.

One minute, I was nursing a second cup of coffee

across from my son in a diner strung with garland and paper snowflakes. The next, I was making plans to stay for the holiday season.

I don't have any upcoming court dates or partner meetings. The only somewhat pressing matters are a few briefs I have due at the beginning of next year, but I can research and write those from anywhere. I haven't taken a real vacation since I made partner. So when Joshua said he knew of a fully furnished short-term rental, I eagerly agreed, telling myself this would be the perfect opportunity to get to know my son better.

But the quiet, inconvenient truth is that I didn't stay just for Joshua.

I stayed because of Claire, too.

Because despite the rational part of my brain telling me to avoid her at all costs, I'm not ready to do that. Not yet. Not after spending the past several weeks hoping my phone would ring and her voice would be on the other end.

The air is crisp and sharp with the scent of cinnamon, pine, and the faintest hint of wood smoke as I step onto the main lawn of Holley Ridge, which looks like even more of a winter wonderland than it did last night.

Tiny white lights spiral around tree trunks. Cobblestone paths are flanked by garland-draped lampposts. Children in knit hats and puffy coats wobble across a pop-up skating rink, their laughter bright and joyful. A line winds toward a gingerbread house, where a very patient Santa poses for photos. Overhead, a jazzy version of "Let It Snow" plays through unseen speakers.

For a moment, I'm no longer forty-two. I'm transported back to my childhood.

Before the sirens.

Before the silence.

Before Christmas became a day of grief and guilt.

"Declan!" Joshua's voice cuts through my memories, and I spot him weaving his way toward me with a huge grin on his face. "You came."

"Why wouldn't I?"

"I figured you'd want to get settled in."

"I can do that later." I pull him in for a quick hug, the gesture still unfamiliar. "After hearing you tell me all about the festival, I needed to see it for myself."

And it *is* something.

Holley Ridge has the kind of charm you see on the covers of puzzle boxes or seasonal cookie tins. The kind of place you don't believe exists until you see it with your own eyes.

And it's not just Holley Ridge, but the entire town. It's exactly like I imagined a small town would be. Friendly. Inviting. Accommodating.

I shouldn't have been able to find a place to stay on such short notice, especially this time of year. Not only is it the annual Holley Ridge Christmas Festival, but Sycamore Falls sits at the foot of a few mountain ranges popular amongst skiers. Short-term rentals are booked over a year in advance.

But Joshua made a few phone calls and, within hours, I was getting settled in my temporary home for the next month.

"It's probably not as classy or sophisticated as the holiday displays in D.C. but—"

"I think it's incredible," I tell him.

He gives me a small smile that mirrors my own. I've only spent a handful of hours with him, but even in that short amount of time, I've seen pieces of myself. Like the square shape of his jaw. The somewhat crooked tilt of his nose. The color of his eyes.

It makes me wonder about other ways I would have influenced him if I'd been a part of his life sooner. And not just genetics, but life lessons. Things I never got from my own father.

"Want something to drink?" Joshua asks. "The local vineyard here is fantastic. Every year, people line up for their mulled wine."

"If it's that popular, I'd hate to miss it."

"This way."

We walk down a path lined with vendor stalls, each one decked out in fake snow and twinkling lights. With each booth I pass, all I can think about is Claire and the role she played in all of this. I wouldn't know where to start planning something like this. Between the vendors, the decorations, not to mention the logistics of parking for the thousands of people here, it's mind-boggling.

Especially since she's so young.

"Did you come here when you were growing up?" I ask in the hopes of getting my mind off the one woman I need to stop thinking about.

"Every year." A small smile tugs at Joshua's lips. "It wasn't nearly this big back then. It all started when Mr. Holley would decorate the house and barn for the holidays, and would allow locals to come walk on their property to see the lights. Mrs. Holley would have hot chocolate for the kids and Irish coffee for the grownups."

"When did it turn into this?"

"It wasn't overnight. Each year, it got bigger and bigger. Now it's one of the most popular Christmas festivals on the west coast. Mom would often volunteer in the craft tent and help little kids make their own ornaments to take home, since she was an art teacher." He laughs under his breath. "I still have every single ornament I made here."

I nod, swallowing the regret that rises in my throat over the reminder of everything I missed. His first word. His first steps. His first day of school.

"I'm sorry I wasn't around for any of it."

A nostalgic gleam fills his gaze. "Do you know what Mom would say to that?"

I don't remember much about Joshua's mom, Hannah. Just that she was a stunning brunette with gorgeous legs and no inhibitions. She was the type of girl every guy would love to spend a few minutes with. And for one night, I was the lucky guy.

"What's that?"

"She'd say you weren't supposed to be around for it. Not because she wouldn't want you to be," he adds quickly. "Mom was a big believer in fate. Said everything happens for a reason. She always felt bad she couldn't tell me more about you, but she was grateful for you. Said you came into her life when she needed you most. Or, I guess, when she needed *me*. Even though she was young, she said having me gave her the direction and structure she needed to get her life on track."

She must have done something right since she managed to raise such an even-headed kid all on her own.

"I still wish I could have been there," I offer.

"You're here now," Joshua offers. "That's all I care about."

It's more grace than I deserve, but I'll take it.

A radio squawks from his jacket pocket, and a muffled voice comes through. Something about a support beam issue in one of the stalls.

"I need to check on that."

"Go," I tell him. "I'm fine."

"The vineyard's booth is at the end of this row. I'll try to catch up with you in a little while."

"Don't worry about me."

With one last smile, he disappears into the crowd, and I'm left to wander the festival on my own. I stop at a booth offering roasted chestnuts, another with handmade ornaments. Someone's giving out samples of peppermint bark. And then I spot the vineyard's booth.

As he mentioned, it's quite popular, and it takes me nearly ten minutes to reach the front of the line. But it's worth it, the warm, spicy flavor like winter in a cup.

I continue to meander through the festival as I sip on my wine, taking in all the sights and smells. A few Christmas markets like this have popped up in D.C. over the years, but I've avoided them like the plague. Hell, I usually avoid anything that even hints at Christmas.

But this is important to Joshua, so now it needs to be important to me.

As I make my way down another row of booths, I spy one selling fudge and start toward it, skirting through the crowds of people. As I do, something slams into me, causing my wine to spill.

I look down, cursing softly at the red stain blooming on my crisp white shirt.

And then I see her.

Claire.

Frozen. Eyes wide. Mouth parted in horror.

"Wha… What are you doing here?" she breathes.

I attempt to shake some of the wine from my fingers.

"Nice to see you again, too."

THIRTEEN

Claire

I blink hard, certain my mind is playing tricks on me.

He can't be here. He was supposed to head back to D.C. today. That's what he said last night.

But there's no mistaking it's him. Declan. Standing in the middle of the Holley Ridge Christmas Festival like a ghost from the one night I've been trying so hard to forget.

Except he's not a ghost. He's real. Solid. Over six feet of muscle and broad shoulders, now wearing a splash of deep red across his white button-down shirt.

"I'm so sorry." I snap out of my stupor, reaching for the front of his shirt like I can somehow make the stain disappear with sheer will. My fingers almost graze his chest before I catch myself. "I wasn't... I didn't see you."

"Don't worry about it." His voice is calm, though there's a flicker of something else beneath the surface. Surprise? Or maybe nerves.

But Declan doesn't seem like the kind of man who gets nervous.

At least he didn't during our one night together.

But I need to stop thinking about *that* Declan.

Instead, I need to only think about him as Joshua's father.

Nothing else.

"I've survived worse," he continues. "Do you mind pointing me to the nearest bathroom?"

"They're in there." I point toward the refurbished barn that now hosts weddings and other important functions. "But it looks like there's more people in that line than the one for Santa."

He scowls at the long line of people snaking along the perimeter.

"You can use the one in my office," I offer before I can think better of it.

"Are you sure?" He raises an eyebrow. "You looked like you were heading somewhere important."

I should take the out he's giving me. Tell him I have too much to do. But just like that night in Boston, there's something about being near him that has me acting out of character.

"I was actually about to head inside," I tell him. "I needed a breather."

"If you're sure?" He arches a single brow.

"It's the least I can do," I respond with a smile, then start toward the building, every inch of me prickling with awareness.

The lobby of the inn is bustling, but it's nowhere near as chaotic as outside. The scent of pine and cinnamon lingers in the air, blending with faint hints of firewood and something sugary.

Declan follows me down the hall, his footsteps echoing against the hardwood floor. The silence between us is thick with tension, everything we shouldn't say hanging in the space between us.

"It's in here." I open the last door on the right and flick on the light.

He steps inside, his eyes sweeping over the room — the window overlooking the lake, desk cluttered with paperwork, bookshelf adorned with several framed photos.

It dawns on me how personal this space is, and I suddenly feel exposed. Like I just let him see a piece of me I never meant to share.

"It's not much, but it's got a great view," I offer nervously. "Especially in the fall. It's my favorite time of year."

"Not Christmas?"

"I love Christmas, but fall..." I push out a sigh.

"It's quieter. Simpler. And the reflection of the trees on the lake with their leaves all different colors is absolutely breathtaking. It's what people should flock here to see." I can't stop the smile that spreads across my face. "But I'm glad they don't."

"Some things are better when you don't invite the world in," he offers.

"Yes, they are."

I slowly bring my eyes to his, and a chill rushes down my spine from the intensity in his gaze. Like I'm a mystery he's desperate to unravel. But it only lasts a heartbeat before he tears his eyes from mine, focusing on one of the framed photos on the bookshelf.

"Is this your sister?" He picks it up, admiring a photo of Genevieve and me from my college graduation.

"It is."

He examines it for a few moments before returning it to the shelf and studying the other photos. I can sense when he spies one of Joshua and me from a yearly camping trip we still go on with several of our friends from high school. His jaw ticks, his shoulders becoming tense.

"You mentioned I could use your bathroom."

"Right." I gesture to the door to the right of the bookcase.

He slides off his suit jacket and drapes it over a chair before loosening and removing his tie. As he steps into the bathroom, he untucks his shirt and grabs a towel. He wets it and brings it up to his shirt.

"I'm not sure that's a good idea," I tell him.

He pauses mid-motion, his eyes finding mine. "What's that?"

"What you're about to do. It'll just set the stain."

"What do you suggest?"

"I can grab some stain remover from housekeeping. I can bring you a shirt, too."

"Do you keep a stash for wine-related emergencies?" he asks with a slight chuckle.

"Our waitstaff wear white dress shirts. I can snag one from the uniform closet. It's probably not the same thread count as yours, but most people around here aren't impressed by designer labels. At least the locals aren't."

"Including you?"

I nod. "Including me."

"A shirt would be great. Thanks."

"Be right back."

I slip into the hallway and take a long, steadying breath. My heart's still racing from the collision. Or maybe just from seeing him again. I thought he'd be gone by now. Thought I could put this entire situation behind me and focus on the Christmas festival.

He's probably just staying through the weekend to spend more time with Joshua. From what I observed last night at dinner, they certainly hit it off. And if

Declan's anything like Joshua, he'd happily rearrange his plans if Joshua asked.

Or even if he didn't.

Once I've found the stain treatment and a clean shirt that looks to be his size, I hurry back to my office. But the instant I cross the threshold, I come to an abrupt stop.

Declan stands shirtless in the middle of the room, turned slightly toward the bookshelf as he studies my photos once more. Warm light spills from the desk lamp, brushing over his tanned skin and illuminating the smattering of tattoos. His back is strong and broad, the muscles shifting subtly as he moves. My gaze trails lower, over the sculpted lines of his torso, the narrow cut of his waist, the dark line of hair leading downward, vanishing beneath the waistband of his pants.

Images of our night together flash before me. Of his body over me. Around me. Inside me. How he drove into me. How he gripped my hips. How he spanked me. The memory is so clear, and before I can stop myself, a soft, traitorous sound escapes my lips.

A moan.

His eyes flick to mine. Dark. Intense. Burning.

He doesn't move. Doesn't speak. Time stands still as the world around us evaporates, the air between us heavy and charged. We're not in my office at Holley Ridge. He's not Joshua's father. We're just two strangers who share an inexplicable connection to each other.

But we *are* in my office. And he *is* Joshua's father. Nothing can change that. Not even an inexplicable connection that seems to get stronger with every second I spend in his presence.

"Here." I thrust the shirt toward him. "It's not exactly tailor-made, but it's better than going shirtless."

He gives me a knowing look, a silent question within, considering he just caught me ogling him.

And he heard the moan to prove it.

"I mean…" I stammer.

"Thanks," he interjects, saving me from having to explain myself.

He takes the shirt from me, his fingers grazing mine. The contact sends a jolt through me, my skin warming from his touch. I spin away, desperate for something else to focus on. *Anything* else.

Spying his stained shirt on my chair, I snatch it and disappear into the bathroom, treating the red mark like it's a medical emergency.

"I thought you were leaving today," I say to cut through the heavy silence.

"I was." I make out the rustle of fabric as he slips the fresh shirt on, but I refuse to steal a peek at him. Not until I know he's fully dressed.

"What happened?"

"This is Joshua's first Christmas without his mom. I figured it might be good for him to have family around. Not sure I qualify as family just yet, but I'm hoping some time together might help toward that end."

A warmth fills me over how hard Declan seems to be trying to have a relationship with Joshua. It restores my faith in humanity that not all fathers are dead-beats. Unlike my own.

"How long are you staying?"

"Probably until after the first of the year."

My breath catches, causing saliva to go down the wrong pipe, and I cough.

"Are you okay with that?"

I snap my head to my left to see him lingering in the doorway, his concerned gaze locked on mine. Thankfully, his sculpted torso is now fully covered.

"Of course," I manage to squeak out once I get my coughing under control. "You don't need my permission to spend time with your son." I return my attention to his shirt, although I'm pretty sure I've already sprayed it enough.

"That's not what I'm talking about, Claire."

"It's fine," I rush out. "Like I said. It was only one night. It didn't mean anything. We'll pretend it never happened."

I can feel him studying me, like he's trying to read between the lines. And maybe he can. Maybe he knows I'm lying through my teeth. That our one night meant more than I thought possible.

But I don't give him the chance to call me out on it.

"Will you be staying with Joshua?" I ask, my tone light and conversational.

"He offered, but I didn't want to intrude since this whole father-son thing is still new to both of us. But he did put me in touch with someone who had a place available."

"You got lucky." I slip past him and grab a hanger off the back of my door, placing the shirt over it to dry. "Short-term rentals are next to impossible this time of year."

"I guess he just moved in with his fiancée and hasn't gotten around to putting it up for rent yet," he states, grabbing his tie and knotting it without looking in a mirror. "He doesn't want to sell because his sister lives in the other half of the duplex."

Alarm bells instantly clang in my head, dread tightening my stomach.

Because Finn, my soon-to-be brother-in-law, just moved in with my sister and he hasn't put his half of the duplex he owns up for rent yet. And his sister, Dylan, my best friend, lives in the other half of the duplex.

With me.

"What's his name? This person you're renting from?"

Declan frowns. "Not sure. He's a firefighter here in town. I haven't had a chance to meet him yet. Joshua arranged it all for me."

I squeeze my eyes shut.

Because Finn's also a firefighter.

"Why do you ask?"

I return my gaze to his.

"Because it looks like we'll be neighbors, Declan."

"That's not possible. Joshua said this guy's sister lives next door."

"She does." I grit a smile. "Her name's Dylan. And she's my roommate."

Silence falls between us as he stares at me like I just told him some horrible truth. Not that we're about to be neighbors.

"Shit. I'm sorry. I'll try to find somewhere else."

But I know he won't find anything. Not within a fifty-mile radius.

Joshua's wondered about his father for years. After everything he's been through over the past several years with taking care of his mother, then losing her, he deserves something good.

"It's okay," I assure him. "I'm barely home anyway. Plus, it's not like we're actually *living* together."

Declan watches me for a long beat. Like he

doesn't believe me. Hell, I'm not sure *I* believe myself, either.

"Seriously, Declan. It's no big deal."

"Are you sure?"

"I am." I force a smile, and another heavy silence falls between us, neither of us knowing what to say.

I'm not sure there *is* anything to say.

"Well…" He clears his throat. "I won't take up any more of your time. Thanks for your help. And the shirt."

"Of course."

He holds my gaze for several long moments, then slips out of my office and into the hallway. Once he disappears from view, I slump into my chair.

It was one thing to pretend that night never happened when he was living on the other side of the country. Out of sight. Out of mind.

But to learn he's not only staying through the holidays, but is my new neighbor?

One thing is certain. This holiday season just got a lot more interesting…

And complicated.

FOURTEEN

Declan

I can't sleep. Not really.

The red numbers on the clock blur every time I roll over. 2:13. 3:27. 4:02. Each minute stretches longer than the last. It's not the unfamiliarity of the bed or the creak of the townhouse settling around me. It's her.

Claire.

Every time I close my eyes, I see her. The way she looked at me in her office mere hours ago. So much heat in her gaze. Like she was ready to forget all the reasons this is a bad idea and beg me to take her against the desk.

God help me, I wanted to. Wanted to erase the distance, fist my hand in her hair, and kiss her until neither of us could breathe. Give myself one last taste.

But I doubt I'd be satisfied with just one last taste.

I'd want more.

And I can't have more.

So I need to settle for nothing. It's the only way.

When the first pale thread of dawn filters through the blinds, I give up on sleep. Shoving back the covers, I plant my feet on the cool hardwood and head into the bathroom. After splashing some water on my face, I change into a pair of running shorts and a long-sleeved shirt. Maybe pounding the pavement will quiet my mind and help me to stop fantasizing about my son's ex.

As I step outside, the crisp morning air hits me, but it's nothing like the frigid temperatures in D.C. this time of year. This is actually quite comfortable. And quiet. If I were back home, the sidewalks would already be teeming with people, even at this early hour.

But here, everything is peaceful. I can make out the soft rumble of a few cars in the distance, along with the occasional barking dog, but other than that, the town is still. Serene. Tranquil.

As I make my way off the porch, I glance to my right. At Claire's townhouse.

There's a wreath on the front door, her porch strung with lights and garland. More lights line the roof and eaves, and there's a Christmas tree in the front bay windows. I smile at the image of Claire decorating her home. Listening to Christmas carols. Maybe even singing along to them.

But then I notice a curtain move in a window on the second floor. I quickly tear my gaze away and take off at a slow pace.

I have no idea where I'm going, but I use the opportunity to explore the small town where my son grew up.

What did he do here as a kid? Did he ride his bike down this same sidewalk? Did he eat ice cream on one of the benches along Main Street? Did he play in the park by City Hall? I want to know. I *need* to know. I missed twenty-four years. Twenty-four birthdays. Twenty-four Christmases.

I'm here to fix that.

But as I wonder what kind of kid Joshua was, thoughts of Claire seep in. Where did he take her on their first date? Did he kiss her goodnight? Did he *more* than kiss her?

I shouldn't be thinking about any of these things. Shouldn't feel anything remotely close to jealousy about my son's ex. But I can't ignore the flash of something raw and uninvited that burns through me at the idea of Joshua being able to hold Claire's hand as they stroll down Main Street in the snow. Or huddle up beneath a blanket as they watch an outdoor movie by the town green. Or share a quiet dinner overlooking the idyllic lake.

Because I can never do these things with her.

It's a surprising thought, since I've never cared to do those things with any woman. My career has been my focus, all my relationships short-lived and meaningless. It's easier that way.

Safer.

But in one night, Claire managed to make me want things I never thought I would.

I pick up the pace, my breath turning ragged as my feet hit the pavement. Harder. Faster. Anything to drown out my thoughts of Claire. I'm here to be a father. That's the only thing that counts. Getting to know my son. Not getting tangled up with the one woman in this town I have no business wanting.

I repeat that like a mantra as I continue running down street after street before eventually winding my way back toward my temporary home.

But when I turn the corner onto the street, I slam directly into someone.

Claire.

Of course.

I catch her by the hips, steadying her before she can stumble. The heat of her skin burns through her clothes, and for a moment, I forget everything I just promised myself.

She's dressed in a pair of dark running shorts that

barely cover the tops of her thighs and a long-sleeved shirt that hugs every damn curve.

Her lips are parted, breath coming fast, and there's that look again. The one that makes me think she's picturing the same thing I am. My mouth on hers. My hands sliding under her shirt. My teeth nipping at her skin, marking her as mine.

I should step back.

I don't.

Not until I realize my thumb is still pressed to her hip, stroking lightly as if it has a mind of its own.

I quickly let go, shoving my hands into my pockets.

"We really need to stop running into each other like this," I say to break the tension.

She blinks, and a quick, nervous smile tugs at her mouth. "Sorry. I wasn't paying attention. Audiobook." She points to her earbuds.

I wonder what kind of book she's listening to. Is it a thriller? Literary fiction? Maybe something historical?

I don't know her well enough to be familiar with her taste in books, but a part of me likes the idea of her listening to a romance novel. When she gets to the steamier parts, would she put me in the hero's place? Would she fantasize about me doing all those things to her?

"I was sort of somewhere else, too. Lost in thought, I guess."

She doesn't press for more information. Just keeps her gaze trained on me, the tension mounting with every damn heartbeat.

Finally, she clears her throat. "I should finish my run so I can get to work."

"Right. Of course." I step back, giving her space.

She jogs past me, her scent invading my senses as she goes, floral and soft. Reminding me yet again of our one night together.

I shouldn't look back. Should keep walking forward.

But lately I've been making a habit out of doing things I shouldn't.

So I turn and watch her run down the street.

Her ponytail swings with each step, her long legs moving in an easy, steady rhythm. And her ass… Hell, that view is lethal in those shorts. I grit my teeth, hating how badly I want to chase after her, consequences be damned.

As if able to sense my stare, she glances over her shoulder, her eyes locking on mine for what feels like an eternity.

Then she looks forward once more, continuing down the street and disappearing around the corner.

By the time she's out of sight, my entire body is tight with frustration. I run the last block like I'm being chased, sprinting up the porch and into the townhouse. Kicking off my shoes, I head straight into the en-suite bathroom.

I turn on the shower and step under the scalding water, desperately trying to erase Claire from my mind.

But it's impossible to erase her… Especially the sight of her in those tiny shorts. The heat in her eyes. The way she bit her bottom lip like she did during our one night.

This is the last thing I should be doing, but I need to do something to release some of this pent-up frustration. With one hand braced against the wall, I wrap my other hand around my erection, moaning Claire's name as I work myself to an orgasm, replaying the memory of her body writhing against mine.

I have a feeling I'll be doing this a lot over the next few weeks.

Especially if I keep running into her like this.

FIFTEEN

Claire

I can't shake the memory of Declan's hand on my hip. The subtle stroke of his thumb against my skin. The chill that consumed me the second he let go.

This is exactly why I went for a run this morning. To stop thinking about him. Not crash straight into him like some rom-com heroine with a head full of fantasy and poor coordination.

I push myself to run faster, welcoming the pain as a distraction. But it's no use. My body still hums, lit like a live wire, every nerve ending buzzing from that single point of contact. I can still feel the heat of him. Can still smell the faint spice of his body wash mixed with the cool, early morning air.

I'd tossed and turned most of the night, consumed

with the idea of Declan being my neighbor. I'd somehow managed to convince myself it wouldn't be a big deal. I barely saw Finn when he lived here. With my busy schedule this time of year, I figured Declan and I would hardly cross paths.

Or maybe I *hoped* we'd hardly cross paths.

It's just my luck that, within hours of learning he's my neighbor, I run into him.

Literally.

Maybe I should talk to him. Get his schedule so we can avoid each other. But that's ridiculous. We're adults. We only spent one night together. One night out of the thousands I've been alive.

Yet it's the one night I can't stop thinking about. The one night that feels branded into my soul. Because for once, I felt like I could be completely free with someone. Someone who wouldn't judge me for my desires. Someone who was eager to give me everything I asked for without hesitation.

Maybe that's the truth of the matter. Maybe it's not necessarily Declan I crave. Maybe I just crave the way he made me feel. Maybe I just need to find someone else who can make me feel the same way. Who I can be free with.

I round the corner onto my street, my lungs burning and my thighs aching. The townhouse comes into view, and a ridiculous wave of nerves tightens in my chest. I slow my pace, glancing at the unit beside mine, feeling like I'm being watched. I hold my breath as I turn onto the walkway leading up to my place, half-expecting the door to Declan's townhouse to swing open.

It doesn't.

Relief floods through me, and I sprint up my porch steps, fumbling to get the key code correct before barging inside like I'm being chased.

Only then do I let myself breathe.

I yank out my earbuds and pause my audiobook. Not that I heard any of it. I ran nearly five miles and can't remember a single thing that happened. All I could think about was *him*.

The grip of his hand on my hips. The way he steadied me. And worse, the way my mind betrayed me by instantly recalling the last time his hands were on my hips, holding me in place as he drove into me like he couldn't get deep enough.

I try to shove the memory down, bury it under thoughts of work deadlines, social media captions, and the dozens of things I need to do today. But my body isn't listening. It's still humming, still aching, still betraying me with every reminder of how alive I felt for those few fleeting seconds.

I wander into the kitchen to find Dylan in the middle of throwing a bunch of fruit into a blender.

"Perfect timing," she says brightly.

She's wearing her usual black chef gear, her

blonde hair smoothed back into a tight ponytail. I grab a glass from the cabinet and fill it with water.

"I was about to shoot you a text to let you know Finn rented out his place. If you see a stranger lurking around over there, it's not someone breaking in."

"Yeah." I take a long sip, forcing my voice to stay even. "He rented to Joshua's father."

Dylan pauses, her hand hovering over the blender as she turns to stare at me. "He's here? Like…living here?"

"Just for the next month." I give a casual shrug. "He wants to spend the holidays getting to know Joshua, especially since this will be his first Christmas without his mom."

"Sounds like a decent guy," she offers.

"He is," I reply quickly, smiling. But it feels stiff, like I'm gritting my teeth.

Her eyes narrow, and I swear for a second she's about to call me out for acting weird. Dylan's been my best friend since we were in diapers. She can read me better than most people, my mom and sister excluded. But before she can pry, she glances at the clock and groans.

"I have to go," she mutters, pouring her smoothie into a travel cup. "The family I'm working for this week needs breakfast before their precious ski day. Pretty sure they think 'personal chef' means 'personal assistant slash nanny.' I can't wait for them to pack up and head back to Beverly Hills." She slings her bag over her shoulder. "Counting down the hours."

I shake my head, wondering how Dylan manages to bite her tongue around some of her uptight clients. She and her friend from culinary school started a personal chef business a few months ago, and while she loves parts of it, some of her clients treat her like hired help rather than a professional chef.

"Before I forget…" Dylan faces me, her keys clutched in her hand. "Are you up for drinks tonight? I need to unwind after a week with these people. If I don't get some bourbon in me soon, I might murder someone with a spatula."

My instinct is to say no. This is one of the busiest weeks of the year at Holley Ridge, and I have a laundry list of things to do. But Parker has unequivocally told me I'm not allowed to work past eight tonight. And staying home means staying here.

Next door to him.

The thought alone makes my skin prickle.

"I could actually use a drink," I respond. "Or ten."

Dylan beams. "Perfect. I'll see you later."

Once she breezes out the door, I head up to my bedroom, strip out of my sweaty clothes, and step under the shower, hoping the hot water will wash away the rest of the tension.

It doesn't.

I close my eyes, letting the steam rise around me, but I still feel him. The press of his body. The weight of his hand. The husky edge in his voice.

A night out with Dylan is exactly what I need. A few drinks with my best friend. A distraction.

Anything to keep me from thinking about the man living on the other side of the wall.

SIXTEEN

Declan

The scent of garlic and rosemary fills the air, mingling with the sound of oil crackling in the pan. I move through the kitchen with the kind of precision I've always found comforting. Not because I'm an expert cook. Far from it. But I've always liked the rules that come with cooking.

Steps. Timers. Predictable outcomes.

In a world full of chaos, it's something I can control.

And control is exactly what I need right now. Something to take my mind off Claire. A reminder of my purpose for being here. To build a relationship with my son.

The doorbell rings just as I'm plating the roasted chicken. I wipe my hands on a towel and head toward the door.

Joshua stands on the porch with a crooked smile and a stack of books tucked beneath one arm. There's an easy confidence about him I envy, as if he doesn't have a care in the world.

"Hope you're hungry." I step aside to let him in.

"If I wasn't before, I definitely am now. It smells amazing."

"Nothing fancy. Just chicken, potatoes, and some sautéed vegetables." I glance at the books as he sets them on the coffee table. "What's all that?"

"Baby books. Mom kept everything." He chuckles softly. "Thought you might want to see them. No pressure, though."

Pressure. The word lingers between us more often than not. Pressure to make up for lost time. Pressure to connect. Pressure not to screw this up.

"I'd like that," I reply and mean it. Hell, I'm the one who should have asked to see photos from his childhood. "But food first."

We settle at the table, and for a while, the only sounds are knives and forks. He murmurs a few quiet compliments between bites, but I can't help feeling uncertain. This is the first time we've truly been alone together. All our previous encounters have been in public with plenty to distract me from the truth that I don't know what to say to my own son. Every move feels uneasy, like navigating a minefield in the dark.

"When we first spoke," he begins after several protracted moments of strained silence, "you mentioned you did an ancestry kit to learn more about your mom's roots?"

I nod, reaching for my glass of wine. "My father never talked about her family. After she died, he shut it all out. Wouldn't answer questions. Wouldn't keep photos up. It was as if she never existed. When he passed away a few years back, it felt like the right time to learn more about her. An ancestry kit seemed like a good place to start."

He nods in understanding, since we both did it in the hopes of getting answers. "How did your mother pass away?"

I swallow hard, the ache I've been carrying since childhood returning. It's dulled over the years, but it never goes away. And it's not out of grief.

Instead, it's out of regret. Blame.

Guilt.

"House fire," I admit softly.

"Shit. I'm sorry. I can't imagine..." He shakes his head, his sympathy more than I deserve. "My mom had cancer, so I had years to prepare, even if it didn't make it any easier. But losing your mom so suddenly like that?"

"It was a long time ago." I manage to sound

neutral, despite the years I've carried the burden of her death.

"Do you have any other family?" he asks cautiously. "Besides your dad?"

"A brother. Miles. He's three years younger. Lives in Florida with his wife and kids."

His eyes light up. "I have cousins?"

The word hits me harder than I expected. I hadn't even thought of that.

"I guess you do."

"How old are they?"

"Lacey is the oldest. She's six. And Nicholas just turned three."

"I'd like to meet them one day. If that's okay," he adds quickly.

I give him a smile. "Of course."

That will require finally telling Miles about the son I never knew I had, something I haven't done yet.

"Are you two close?" Joshua asks, bringing a potato up to his mouth.

"Not as close as we were when we were growing up. The downside of getting older, I suppose. Still, he knows he can always call when he needs me. And I can call him, too."

"That's nice. That's sort of who Claire's always been to me."

At the mention of her name, a renewed wave of

guilt washes over me, and I do my best to school my expression.

"How long have you known her?" I take a sip of wine, wishing it were stronger.

I still have so many questions about their relationship. He didn't go into too much detail the other night, just that they were once more than friends before realizing it was a mistake.

"We went to preschool together. Over the years, she sort of became the sibling I never had."

"How did you go from being friends to…more than friends?" I ask around the sour taste in my mouth.

"Hormones, mostly," he says with a laugh.

"Hormones?" My stomach tightens, but I force my face to remain neutral.

"Claire had a crush on a different guy in our grade, and he asked her out, but she was kind of nervous since she'd never even kissed someone. So being the good friend I am, I offered to help her practice. On me."

I'm not sure who I'm more jealous of. This nameless person who caught Claire's attention, or my own son.

"And did she?"

"She did."

"And the other guy?"

"Was a dick to her." His jaw tenses, and I can feel his anger, despite how long it's been since this happened. It reminds me of myself.

"So did you ask her out after that?"

"No. In fact, I don't think I ever really asked her out."

"You didn't?" I scrunch my brows.

"We'd still…practice with each other, but always with the expectation of eventually dating someone else. We were simply friends who hooked up. Until…"

"Yes?"

He blows out a self-deprecating laugh. "Until I asked her to marry me last year."

I nearly spit out my chicken, his statement taking me completely by surprise. "You what? I didn't think you were serious."

It was one thing for them to sleep together. But for him to ask her to *marry* him?

"We weren't," he answers

"Then…"

"Mom was sick." He finishes chewing a piece of chicken and washes it down with some wine. "When her last round of chemo didn't work like she'd hoped and she opted out of additional treatment, I don't know…" He blows out a long breath. "I guess I thought it would bring my mom some joy in her final few months."

I nod. If I were in his shoes, I probably would have done the same thing.

"Thankfully, Claire saw it for what it was and turned me down."

"And now?"

"We're back to being friends."

"Just friends?" I ask, needing confirmation I didn't fuck Claire while he still was.

"Yes." He laughs. "Just friends. No more benefits. We agreed we never should have crossed that line."

"And you're okay with that?" I press.

"I wouldn't want it any other way. There was never that…spark. For either of us."

I consider his story for several long moments, unsure how to feel about his relationship with the woman I haven't been able to stop thinking about. In a way, it provides me with a certain level of comfort that there were never any romantic feelings between them. But she's still my son's friend.

She's still off limits.

"Did you grow up in the D.C. area?" Joshua asks, changing the subject.

"Connecticut, actually."

"I have to ask. Red Sox or Yankees?"

"Red Sox. I was a fan when they kept choking in the playoffs."

"That must have been painful."

"It sure was," I say with a laugh.

He continues to ask questions about anything that pops into his head as we finish our meal, and I'm more than happy to talk about something other than Claire.

After we're done and I've cleaned the kitchen, I join Joshua on the couch in the living room.

"Do you mind if I look through some of these?" I pick up one of the baby books.

"It's why I brought them."

I open the book to the first page. It's covered in photos from the hospital, his tiny fingers wrapped around Hannah's thumb as she holds him close.

"She loved these books," Joshua says from beside me as I flip through the pages, each one documenting different milestones. "Told me she was worried she'd forget something if she didn't write it all down."

Page after page, I watch my son's life unfold in faded snapshots and handwritten notes. His first steps. His favorite toys. Finger-painted birthday cards. It's a strange thing, seeing your own child grow up in fast-forward, knowing you weren't part of it. But it doesn't make it less meaningful.

"She really loved you," I murmur as I admire a photo of Joshua and his mother when he was around six. They were on a boat, their skin sun-kissed, their smiles wide.

"I was lucky."

I turn another page, wanting to know everything I can about Joshua's childhood, and my breath catches.

There's a photo of two kids in puffy jackets, standing in front of a snowman. One of them is unmistakably Joshua, all crooked grin and missing teeth. The other is Claire.

Her hair's pulled into two braids, and she beams at the camera like she owns the world, her arm slung around Joshua's shoulders. Even at that age, the connection between them is obvious.

It's one thing to listen to him talk about their life-long friendship.

It's another to see it for myself.

And I'm the asshole who keeps fantasizing about my son's best friend.

I clear my throat and sit back, suddenly needing more space. "Thanks for bringing these. For letting me see all of this. And not hating me for not being there."

"I told you last night." Joshua closes the book and sets it on the table. "You're here now. That's all that matters. And I'm really glad you *are* here, Declan. It means a lot."

"I remember my first Christmas after I lost my mother. It was…awful. I didn't want you to feel alone."

"Is that how you felt?"

I shouldn't have felt that way. I was with my

brother. And my father was there physically, even if he spent it with a bottle in his hand, looking at me like he couldn't stand the sight of me. But I've learned it's possible to be surrounded by people and still feel alone.

"I did."

He nods, not pressing for more information. "Well, thank you for being here."

"Of course."

He checks the time and sighs, slowly pulling himself to his feet. "I should get going. Early morning tomorrow. If you want, I can leave these here so you can look through them." He gestures toward the books.

"I'd like that."

I rise to my feet and walk him to his car, the cold night air brushing against my skin as we step outside. He's halfway down the steps when the door to the townhouse beside mine opens and Claire walks out with a petite blonde, both of them dressed in jeans and somewhat revealing tops.

Claire spots me instantly and freezes, her eyes locked on mine as if unable to look away. My jaw tightens as I take in the curve of her hips, focusing on the sliver of skin where her top rides up. She looks like sin and salvation wrapped into one confusing, infuriating package.

Thankfully, Joshua doesn't seem to notice me eye-fucking his best friend. Instead, he grins and walks over to her, wrapping her in a hug.

"You two going out?"

"We are," the blonde says. "I've had the client from hell all week and need a damn drink. So does she." She hooks her thumb at Claire, then shifts her attention toward me. "You must be Joshua's father. Claire mentioned you're renting my brother's place."

Joshua turns toward Claire. "I didn't think I'd told you yet."

"We ran into each other this morning when I went for a run." She smiles nonchalantly as a car pulls up to the curb. "That's our ride."

"Don't get into too much trouble tonight," Joshua says with a wink.

"No promises," Claire retorts.

"Text me when you get home so I know you're safe. Okay?"

"Of course."

He places a soft kiss on her cheek, and I clench my fists over the idea of him being able to feel her perfect skin while all I can do is watch.

I'm about to offer to take them wherever they're going myself so she doesn't have to get into the car with a complete stranger, but I don't. It's not my place.

Instead, I remain silent as she climbs into the back

seat, her eyes briefly meeting mine before she closes the door.

I steal a glance at Joshua as we both watch the car pull away.

There's no doubt in my mind.

We're both thinking about the same thing.

We're both thinking about Claire.

Except he's just thinking about her as a friend.

And I'm thinking about her in a way I shouldn't.

SEVENTEEN

Claire

By the time Dylan and I slide into a booth in the corner of the bar, I've already downed half my martini. I can't get it into me fast enough. The alcohol goes down smooth, but my nerves stay jagged. My cheeks are hot, my pulse still racing from seeing Declan again.

The way he looked at me... So much heat. So much want.

Just like he did in Boston.

Like he was the first person to ever really see me.

"To surviving the week." Dylan's lifts her glass containing her old fashioned.

I raise my martini and clink it against hers. "To surviving the week," I echo.

Between finding out the man I spent a night tangled up with is Joshua's dad, then learning he's not only staying in town but will be my neighbor for the next month, survival feels like a pretty low bar to clear.

I take a swallow of my drink, the alcohol burning a trail down my throat, and allow my gaze to wander the room.

The place is buzzing tonight. The air is warm, heavy with the scent of fried food and spilled beer, the speakers pumping out a mix of classic rock and holiday covers. Gold and silver strings of garland glitter from the rafters as colored lights blink in a lopsided rhythm, making even this rowdy little bar past the town limits feel festive.

"Okay." Dylan sets her drink down, pulling my attention back to her. "I'm just going to come right out and say it."

"Say what?" I ask nervously, fearing the worst.

She leans closer, her brows raised in a knowing look.

I bring my martini back to my lips, though it sloshes over the rim from the subtle tremble in my hand.

"Joshua's dad."

I choke a little on my drink, but push it down. "What about him?"

She smirks, a wicked glint in her eye. "Oh, come on. I think you know."

My heart hammers in my chest, heat creeping up my neck. I shouldn't be surprised. Dylan's always had an ability to read between the lines. It wouldn't take her long to pick up on the tension between Declan and me. The way we had to physically force ourselves to look away from each other.

I open my mouth, searching my brain for the words I need, when she blurts out, "He's fucking hot."

I blink, both relieved and confused. "What?"

"I mean, sure, he's Joshua's dad, but holy shit, Claire. That voice? That beard? And those eyes?" She fans herself dramatically. "I bet he has tattoos. He seems like the type. All polished on the outside, with a bad boy streak a mile long."

I fight my smile as I relax into the booth. She's not that far off. He does have tattoos. And he definitely has a bad boy streak, too. Especially in the bedroom.

"Tell me you don't find him hot. I dare you. That man puts the fox in silver fox."

"He's not all that silver, though."

Dylan shrugs, sipping her drink. "I noticed a few flecks of gray. It's silver enough for me." She winks.

"Silver foxes?" a cheerful voice cuts in before I can respond. "Did I come at the right time?"

A petite brunette places a rocks glass on the table before sliding into the booth beside Dylan.

"You certainly did," Dylan says with a subtle waggle of her brow. "Claire, this is Rowan. Rowan, this is my roommate, Claire."

Rowan extends her hand toward me, and we shake. "Nice to meet you."

"Rowan is Hayden's new nanny."

I nearly choke on my drink yet again.

I knew Dylan was no longer taking care of her brother's kids, not with all the hours she's working. I figured her mother was happy to watch them. To learn he actually hired a nanny when he's been vehemently against it completely floors me.

Hayden can be...difficult, to say the least. After all, he's still grieving the loss of his wife last year. Not that it gives him the right to be an asshole. Then again, I'm not sure I'd call him an asshole. Just someone who's a bit lost right now and is taking his grief out on the world.

"How's that going?" I ask Rowan with a single brow arched.

"Why do you think I'm here?" she retorts with a smile, raising the glass to her lips and taking a sip. "The man sent me a spreadsheet with a list of approved and prohibited snacks. And he wants to put tracking devices on me and the kids so he knows where we are at all times."

"Hayden can definitely be intense," Dylan adds.

"And bossy. Overbearing. Infuriating." Rowan

rolls her eyes before her expression softens. "But I understand where he's coming from. He lost his wife and is trying to figure out life without her. That can't be easy."

I notice a flicker of something in her eyes, an underlying affection that goes beyond her just being the nanny.

I get a feeling Dylan picks up on it, too, her brows scrunched as she studies Rowan curiously.

But before she can question her, Rowan straightens, her smile brightening.

"Enough about me and *my* problems." She faces Dylan. "How was your day? Your own client from hell?"

Dylan groans. "Don't get me started. This woman has been an absolute nightmare. They gave me a menu. A *menu.* Like I'm a line cook, not a trained chef."

She launches into a rant about how controlling the woman is, often hovering over her in the kitchen in a way that makes Gordon Ramsay look like a preschool teacher. Thankfully, most of her clients don't bother her. They give her a list of allergies and dietary restrictions, and she plans the menu. But not these people, it seems. These people want control.

"But next week's clients sound better," she adds, relaxing slightly. "Laid back. One of them has celiac, which comes with its own challenges, but at least they're not micromanaging me. And they seem to have quite varied tastes. There are a few dishes I've been wanting to try out, and they might be some good guinea pigs."

I settle into the booth, listening to Dylan tell me about some of her ideas for the coming week. It's a nice distraction from thinking about Declan, which is exactly what I need. Why I agreed to come out in the first place.

But as she tells me about possibly hiring more staff to meet the increasing demand, something prickles at the back of my neck. That awareness again.

The kind that sets my skin on edge before my brain has a chance to catch up.

I try to ignore it. Blame it on the alcohol. But when it won't go away, I steal a glance over my shoulder, stiffening when I see Declan sitting at the bar.

He's dressed in the same charcoal gray sweater he was wearing earlier that hugs his physique as if it was woven just for him. He sits at the bar as he sips an amber liquid with an unreadable expression on his face.

Damn him for being so handsome.

For making me want him when I'm not supposed to.

For treating me to one of the best nights of my

life, then turning out to be the one man I can never have.

He starts to shift his gaze around the bar, and I snap my gaze back to Dylan and Rowan before he sees me.

"Want to play pool?" I rush out.

"You hate playing pool," Dylan retorts.

"I don't *hate* it. I'm just bad at it."

"Right," she draws out, giving me that look again. The one that says she knows something's up but is choosing not to press. For now, anyway.

"I wouldn't mind playing," Rowan offers.

"Great," I say, already sliding from the booth, clutching my martini like a lifeline.

The pool tables are at the far end of the bar, shadows pooling under neon lights. I busy myself with racking the balls, focusing on the clatter and click instead of the pulse hammering in my chest.

But the moment I line up my first shot, I feel it again.

That magnetic pull.

I lift my gaze, and there he is. Watching me from across the room. His eyes locked on mine.

Deep blue.

Unblinking.

Searing.

Like no one else exists.

EIGHTEEN

Declan

I should be asleep.

Instead, I'm nursing my second scotch at a bar on the outskirts of Sycamore Falls, wondering what the hell is wrong with me.

I came here to get out of my head. To stop thinking about Claire. I couldn't do that in my townhouse. Not when photos of her filled the books Joshua left for me. It shouldn't have surprised me. It's obvious how close they were.

How close they *are*.

But those photos solidified it in living color.

Birthday parties. School concerts. Tree forts. Joshua's childhood frozen in time.

And Claire was in so many of them.

With grass stains on her jeans and birthday cake on her face. In a soccer uniform, standing shoulder-to-shoulder with Joshua, both smiling and red-faced after a game. In a swimsuit at the lake, her arms flung around Joshua, laughing like she didn't have a care in the world.

They've known each other practically since birth. She's been a fixture in his life for years now. She's not just a friend. She's his constant.

And I can't stop thinking about how goddamn perfect her body felt against mine.

Which is why I needed to go somewhere without the persistent reminders of her and her connection to my son. I figured a bar far away from downtown Sycamore Falls would be safe.

Clearly, the universe has a sense of humor, because this is where she ended up. I should have left the second I met her eyes from across the room.

But I didn't.

Instead, I stayed, torturing myself and watching her in a darkened corner of the bar like an obsessed stalker. I try to look away as she bends over the pool table, her dark hair tumbling over one shoulder as she lines up a shot. But I can't.

I'm not the only one who's noticed her, either. A group of guys lingering nearby are watching her, their eyes tracking her every move. One of them nudges another and jerks his chin in her direction, clearly trying to help him work up the nerve to go over.

He eventually does, despite my muttered curses and threats that he keep his distance. The music is too loud for me to hear their conversation, but it's obvious he's asking if they can join their game.

And Claire agrees.

I reach for my wallet, needing to get out of this place before I do something I'll regret.

Then I hear it. Her laughter floating through the room. It's bright and unguarded, the kind of laugh that turns heads… Including mine.

When I look her way this time, she angles her body a little too close to the guy in the button-down for my liking. He passes her a cue, brushing her arm as he does. It's casual. Innocent. And yet when Claire tucks her hair behind her ear and smiles at him, I'm overcome with a jealousy I've never experienced before. Even worse than watching Joshua touch her. Because I know they're just friends.

This guy, though? She could go home with him if she wants.

Worse, she could bring *him* home with her.

Which is probably why I want to break his jaw.

I stare down at the amber liquid in my glass, telling myself to walk away. Be the adult. Be *sane*.

But then I notice movement in my periphery and watch as Claire disappears down the hallway.

I'm out of my chair before I can think better of it, heading toward the same corridor just as the door to the women's restroom swings shut.

I lean against the wall and stare at the scuffed floor, trying to pull myself together. Come up with some sort of rationale for what I'm doing. But there isn't one.

All the more reason I should turn around right now before Claire sees me waiting outside the ladies' room.

But I don't have a chance before the door opens.

Claire steps into the hallway and freezes when she sees me. Her eyes go wide, hand flying to her chest.

"Jesus," she breathes. "You scared me."

"Do you want him?" I demand.

Her brows knit together. "What?"

"That guy you've been flirting with. Do. You. Want. Him?"

She crosses her arms, lifting her chin in defiance. "Maybe."

I narrow my eyes. "I don't believe you."

She doesn't respond right away. Just glares at me like she wants to both slap me and kiss me at the same time.

Then her expression softens, showing a vulnerability I didn't expect. "Maybe I just want to forget you."

The words hit harder than they should, leaving me momentarily speechless.

"Is that why you're flirting with him?" I take a cautious step toward her. "To forget me?"

She gives a small nod of her head.

"And have you?" My gaze drops to her mouth.

"No."

Relief hits me hard and fast. My pulse pounds as I press one hand to the wall beside her, caging her in. The scent of her body wash curls around me — vanilla and spice, warm and infuriatingly addictive.

"But I need to," she adds, yet doesn't attempt to retreat. If anything, she leans into me even more.

"Why?"

"We both know why."

"I don't think I can ever forget you, Claire." I edge closer still, regardless of every single reason I shouldn't be here.

I know this is wrong. Know I should walk away right now, but I hate the idea of anyone else knowing the side of Claire I was lucky enough to have for one night.

"The way you move. The way you feel. The way you taste."

She closes her eyes as a tiny whimper escapes her throat.

"It's permanently imprinted in my mind."

"It was just one night," she whispers, repeating the

same line I've heard more times than I can count. The same line I've told myself more times than I can count.

But tonight, it doesn't seem like a reminder.

Instead, it seems like a challenge, especially as her body betrays her words, her hips shifting closer, head tilting back, lips parting like she's waiting for me to take what we both want.

From the moment I first laid eyes on her, she cast a spell on me. I had a feeling once I had a taste, I'd never be satisfied with anyone else. It wasn't just the sex. It was the trust she put in me as she shared her deepest desires.

The trust she put in me to give her what she craved.

"It wasn't just one night," I growl. "And you know it."

She licks her lips and arches closer still, her mouth nearly skimming mine. It sends a wave of electricity through me, my body throbbing with need.

Then the sound of footsteps cuts through, snapping us back to reality.

Claire jumps away from me just as Dylan rounds the corner

"Oh." She comes to an abrupt stop when she sees us. "Declan. I didn't realize you were here."

"I guess we have the same taste in bars," I say, forcing my eyes away from Claire.

"I was just giving Declan a few ideas for Joshua's Christmas gift," Claire offers without prompting. "I guess I got carried away."

"Right," Dylan draws out, floating her suspicious gaze between us, as if trying to put together a puzzle.

"I'll be right out," Claire offers.

Dylan continues to scrutinize us for several more nerve-wracking seconds. Then she levels Claire with a look I can't quite read. "It's your turn, so hurry back."

"I will."

Once we're alone again, Claire pushes out a long exhale before turning her fiery eyes toward me.

"This…" She gestures between us, "can't happen again."

I push out a breath and run my fingers through my hair. "I know."

Even though nothing *did* happen. If Dylan hadn't interrupted, something very well could have.

"I'll let you get back to your friends." I increase the space between us, hating to let her go, but I don't have a choice. "I'm sorry for my behavior. You should feel free to flirt with whomever you want."

She gives a subtle nod, then spins around, slowly making her way back to her friends. But just before she turns the corner, she glances over her shoulder and meets my gaze one last time. She parts her lips, as if she wants to say something. But she doesn't.

Instead, she shakes her head before disappearing from view.

NINETEEN

Claire

The gravel crunches beneath my tires as I pull into the lot at McKinley's Tree Farm. The scent hits me the moment I step out of my car, a breath of something sharp and fresh, like it's trying to clear away the clutter in my head. If only it were that easy.

The wind nips at my cheeks as I make my way toward the barn to pick up the centerpieces Mrs. McKinley is donating for the kids' holiday carnival this week. Frost sparkles like crushed glass along the wooden fence posts, the sun barely clearing the tops of the trees. I tug my coat tighter around myself, willing the cold to drown out the thoughts still buzzing like static in the back of my brain.

It's been over a week since the bar. Since Declan.

Since he hovered over me, his lips a breath from mine.

I haven't seen him since I walked away from him in that darkened bar. Not at Holley Ridge. Not during my morning runs. Not even when Dylan, Rowan, and I went out for drinks again this past weekend to the same bar. I'd be lying if I said the chance of seeing him there again didn't factor into my decision.

But he wasn't there.

I haven't so much as peeked a glimpse of him as I've stared out my bedroom window like a deranged peeping Tom.

I hate how much I miss him.

Hate how I can't stop thinking about him.

Hate how my body aches with the memory of his touch.

Hate all the nights I've spent with my hand between my thighs.

Hate how I've whispered his name in the dark like it's a secret I can't stop telling.

Hate how I've replayed our one night together as I made myself come.

My cheeks heat from the memory, and I quickly brush it off, focusing on why I'm here. Centerpieces. Carnival. Mrs. McKinley.

But as I pass the rows of pre-cut trees, I notice a

familiar figure standing between a few eight-foot Noble Firs.

Declan.

He looks out of place here, surrounded by flannel and fleece and family chaos. His shoes are too pristine, his coat too expensive, his pants too starched.

But it's not just his clothes that make him look foreign. It's the way he moves. There's an air of control about him. A quiet intensity that makes him feel separate. Removed. Like he's not part of this world but is desperately trying to figure out how to walk through it without anyone noticing.

It makes me want to peel back his cold outer shell and bring back the man I spent a few hours with during a snowstorm in Boston.

But I can't. Not when he's Joshua's father.

So I try to hurry past, pretending not to notice him.

As I do, he lifts his head and our eyes lock. His gaze softens the moment it lands on me, but he still doesn't smile. Not really. Instead, there's a flicker of something else. Something warm that sparks in his expression. But just as quickly, his mouth tightens.

"I can come back later," he says, his voice colder than I remember. He turns, starting toward the parking lot.

"You don't need to leave because of me," I call after him, and he pauses, glancing back toward me. "I won't be long. Just picking up a few things for Holley Ridge."

"Are you sure?"

"It's fine," I reply, forcing a smile. "Really."

He fully faces me, and I feel like I should say something more. What is there to say?

Instead, I turn from him and head toward the barn, trying to shake off the tension I feel deep in my chest.

Inside, the scent of pine and cinnamon swirls through the warm air. Handmade wreaths line the walls, their red bows bright against the worn wood. Strings of white lights blink lazily overhead, intertwined with garland. It looks and smells like every Christmas memory I've ever loved, reminding me of coming here every year with my mother and sister to pick out a tree. But those memories don't comfort me like they once did.

Because now all I can think about is Declan.

"Claire Thomas," a familiar voice calls out, full of warmth.

I snap my head up as Mrs. McKinley bustles out from behind the counter, her arms open and inviting.

"It's so nice to see you, sweetie."

"You, too."

"Don't tell me you went fake on me," she chastises with a subtle look of scorn. "I haven't seen you at the farm yet to get a tree."

"I'd never do that to you," I assure her. "I've been working so much with the Christmas Festival and all, so I let Dylan take care of it."

"That's good. And how are your mom and sister?"

"Great. Gen just found out she's having a girl."

She covers her heart with her hand. "She must be over the moon." Then she leans closer. "I always knew she and Finn would get together someday."

I laugh. "I think we all did."

"Well, I know you're not here to update me on the town gossip. Let's get those centerpieces for you."

"Thanks, Mrs. McKinley. Your donation means a lot."

"You know I'm always happy to help when I can." She heads toward the open door of the barn. "Theo! Can you help Claire bring the centerpieces to her car?"

"He doesn't have to. I can manage myself."

"Nonsense." She waves me off. "He has to earn his paycheck some way," she says with a wink, since Theo is her son and will be taking over the tree farm one day.

Theo McKinley appears in the open doorway, wiping his hands on a cloth. He's always been handsome in a rugged, salt-of-the-earth kind of way.

"Hey, Claire," he greets with a heartwarming smile.

"Good to see you, Theo."

He easily lifts the three boxes containing the centerpieces like they weigh nothing, refusing to let me carry a single one. I lead him toward my SUV as we talk about the festival, my position at Holley Ridge, both of us commiserating about all the long hours we've been working this time of year.

Once he's done loading the boxes, he leans against the side of my car and crosses his arms in front of his chest. It pulls his flannel shirt tight, and I sense he's trying to show off. One thing is certain. The years he's spent hauling trees have certainly paid off.

"Any chance you'd want to grab a drink after the holidays when things slow down?" he asks, treating me to the same smile that made my stomach flip when I was a teenager. "We can decompress a bit."

A few weeks ago, I would've said yes without hesitation. He's kind. Has an incredible work ethic. Wants a family. He's rooted here. All the things I've always wanted.

Except now I want them with someone who is off limits in every meaning of the word.

But I can't keep pining for something that can never be.

Plus, it's only a drink. Not a marriage proposal.

"I'd like that," I say, although my voice lacks any sort of enthusiasm.

He beams. "Great. I'll call you."

"Sounds good."

He gives me one last smile before jogging off to help tie a tree onto someone's car. I watch him for several long moments, trying to muster some sort of excitement at the prospect of going on a date with Theo McKinley, something teenage me would have lost sleep over.

But I can't.

With a long sigh, I open my car door, stealing one last glance at the tree farm. Couples and families meander through row after row of trees, parents letting their kids tug them toward the biggest one they can find.

And then there's Declan. Alone. Staring at a tree as if it's some foreign object.

He looks like he's wandered into someone else's family photo and doesn't quite know whether he should be a part of it.

It makes my heart squeeze, and before I can talk myself out of it, I close my door and head back to the tree farm, my boots crunching over frostbitten needles and leaves.

Declan doesn't immediately look up when I approach. He seems lost in thought, his hands buried in his pockets, his shoulders hunched like the cold has finally found its way through that polished exterior. I've never seen him like this. So…sad.

"Would you like some company?" I offer.

He snaps his eyes toward mine, completely taken aback by my presence.

"You look like you're a bit out of your depth here." I push out a laugh, hoping to cut through the tension.

He blinks repeatedly, as if clearing whatever he was just thinking about from his mind.

Then he blows out a long breath, the stiffness in his posture gradually waning.

"I could definitely use some help."

TWENTY

Declan

Claire walks beside me, her gloved hands stuffed into the pockets of her oversized puffy coat. Her breath clouds in the air, her cheeks flushed a deep pink from the cold.

I keep my eyes trained forward, unsure how to act around her.

Actually, that's not entirely true. I know how I should act. Friendly. Detached. Uninterested. Like she's my son's best friend and nothing more.

Like I haven't spent the past several weeks craving the feel of her legs wrapped around my waist.

Like I haven't longed to hear the sound she makes when she comes.

Like I haven't jerked off to the memory of her pussy clenching around me every damn day.

Sometimes twice.

I should have declined her offer of help. Nothing good can come from spending time with her.

But Claire has this gravity around her that keeps pulling me into her orbit.

"Let me guess..." Her teasing voice cuts through the awkward silence as we meander through the rows of trees. "You're more the artificial tree type. And not just a plain artificial tree, either. You get one with the lights already attached so you don't have to deal with testing them and cursing when they inevitably don't work, even though they were fine the year before."

I chuckle, my lips curving up at the corners. "It sounds like you're speaking from experience."

"With regard to an artificial tree, absolutely not. I love the smell of a real tree."

She inhales a deep breath, her eyes briefly closing as she basks in the scent of pine and cedar that permeates this place. She looks so happy. So carefree.

I wish I could find joy in the smell of Christmas trees.

Instead, it brings forward memories of that night. Of the scorching heat. The burning in my lungs.

The blame.

"But testing lights?" she continues. "Definitely. I'm

pretty sure the manufacturers intentionally make it so their product only works for one season."

"It wouldn't surprise me," I say with a smile, before looking forward once more.

"So am I right? You have a fake tree, don't you?"

"Truthfully, I haven't had a tree in years. Not since I was a boy."

"What?" She comes to an abrupt stop, staring at me like I just confessed to some horrific crime. Like kicking puppies for fun.

In her mind, I may as well have.

"Declan," she begins, her tone scandalized. "Christmas without a tree is like…" She shakes her head, searching for the right words. "It's like a peanut butter and jelly sandwich without the peanut butter and jelly."

I arch a brow. "So…just bread."

"Exactly. Sad and pointless, at least when you could have peanut butter and jelly with it. Why haven't you put up a tree? Are you secretly a Grinch? Do you hate Christmas or something?"

"I don't hate Christmas," I reply, continuing along the rows of trees. "I've been alone for most of my adult life. The only person around to enjoy a tree is me, and I'm perfectly happy without one."

"You don't have any family?" She steals a glance at me as I look straight ahead, unsure how we went from picking out a Christmas tree to peeling back the armor I've always kept firmly in place. "Apart from Joshua, of course," she adds quickly.

As if I need a reminder of the reason I can never touch her.

"I have a brother."

"Are you two not close?"

"We are, I suppose."

"Then you're not *really* alone," she offers softly. "You just choose to be."

The words hit harder than I expected, and I stop walking once more. I glance at Claire, but she's examining a tree like she didn't gut me with a single sentence.

Like she didn't *see* me in a way no one else ever has.

I can't deny she has a point.

After my mother died, after the accusations and guilt and blame, I told myself it was safer this way. Keep everyone out. Don't risk being needed. Don't risk failing someone ever again.

I thought I could survive like that.

But then Claire walks into my life, bright and warm and uncomplicated. She makes it harder to stay numb. Harder to pretend I've been content in this quiet, empty life I built.

"What about you?" I clear my throat, desperate for a change of subject. "Are you close to your family?"

"My sister's my best friend. But don't tell Dylan." She winks conspiratorially.

"And your parents?"

"My mom's great, even if a bit…eccentric at times."

"What about your dad?"

Claire shrugs, her expression falling. "He left when my mom was eight months pregnant with me."

"Jesus," I exhale, unsure what I expected her to say. It wasn't this.

It takes a special kind of asshole to abandon his kids. I feel like enough of a prick for not being there for Joshua until now, even though I had no idea he even existed. But to walk away from your family?

It's not that far off from what my father did after Mom died. He may have been there physically, but that was the extent of it. He no longer felt like a father to me.

"I… I'm so sorry, Claire. That's… He's a fucking idiot."

She shrugs again, but it's tighter this time. "It messed up my sister more. She was six when he left. But me? I never knew him. It's kind of hard to miss someone you never met."

I study her face. There's a flicker there. Something unsaid. She's not as unaffected as she wants me to believe. I recognize that deflection too well. I've spent most of my life doing the same thing.

"My mom always said it was his loss since both of her daughters are awesome."

I let out a low chuckle. "I don't know your sister, but based on what I know about you, I can definitely attest to that." I slow my steps and fully face her. "I couldn't imagine ever walking away from you. Not willingly anyway."

Her gaze lifts to mine and, for a beat too long, we just look at each other.

The cold disappears. So does the noise around us. I shouldn't say shit like this. But it's the truth. Claire's one of the most amazing women I've met in a long time. Not only is she beautiful, but she's also compassionate. She has a presence about her that lights up any room she walks into.

"What made you change your mind?" she asks, breaking the moment before it can build into something we can't take back. She faces forward once more, her eyes focused anywhere but on me.

"What do you mean?"

"Why get a tree now?"

"Joshua, I suppose. I want to give him a good Christmas. Make up for the ones I missed. I just want this Christmas to be memorable. Or, at the very least, not as difficult for him as it could be. I want it to be what he's used to."

"It doesn't need to be perfect. Or the kind of

Christmas he always had with his mom. Just give him *you*. Give him a Declan Christmas."

I snort. "That would mean working sixteen hours and relishing the silence in the office with everyone gone."

She comes to another abrupt stop and stares at me, looking even more horrified than she did about me never putting up a tree. "You *work* on Christmas?"

"What else am I going to do?"

"I don't know!" She throws up her hands in exasperation. "Spend it with your brother maybe?"

"He lives in Florida."

"Florida isn't *that* far from D.C."

I sigh, dragging a hand over my face. "I guess I always feel...out of place. He's married. Two kids. Their life feels...full. And I..." I hesitate, the words stuck in my chest.

How do I explain this to her without revealing the truth? That every time I contemplate celebrating Christmas with his family, all I'll be able to think about is how it's my fault my mother isn't there to play with her grandkids or spoil them with presents.

It's why I don't celebrate Christmas.

Instead, I bury myself in work to forget. But the guilt never really fades.

It hasn't in over thirty years. I doubt it ever will.

"I guess I don't want to feel like a burden," I finally say, shoving my hands into my pockets.

"I may not know your brother," Claire begins cautiously, "but if you're as close as you say, he'd never see you that way. He probably just wants his brother around."

"I'm not usually great company. Especially around the holidays."

"I like your company." She slows to a stop and faces me, her eyes finding mine. "I probably shouldn't admit this, but I've missed your company."

The air between us shifts again. Thickens. Warms.

This entire scene feels straight out of a Christmas card. Or a holiday movie. Surrounded by Christmas trees. A woman who lives and breathes Christmas helping a miserly grump like me pick out a tree. Holiday music piped in through the speakers. Maybe it's being in this place that has me acting out of character. Or finally sharing pieces of myself I've kept locked up for years.

"You're right," I say softly. "You probably shouldn't admit that."

"Do you want me to take it back?" she asks.

"No," I reply, my eyes dropping to her lips. So full. So soft.

And the way they moved against mine… God. I shouldn't be thinking about her like this. Shouldn't be remembering that night. Shouldn't be remembering how warm her mouth felt on every inch of my body, but I can't help it.

So instead of keeping my distance like I promised myself I would, I lean closer.

Out of nowhere, a toddler runs past us, bumping into Claire and nearly causing her to lose her balance.

I steady her, the feel of her body against mine just as intoxicating as it was the last time I touched her. But she quickly scrambles out of my hold.

"You should get this one." She nods toward the tree in front of us. "It has a bit of a lean, but they can level it out for you."

"Right," I respond, pushing down any hint of disappointment. "Thanks for your help."

"Of course." She grits a smile, then turns away, hurrying down the row of trees.

"Claire," I call out before she disappears from view.

She pauses, meeting my eyes from over her shoulder.

"I shouldn't say this either, but I've missed your company, too."

Her lips curve in that same teasing smile that undid me in Boston.

Then she walks away.

And I'm pretty sure she sways her hips a little more than usual.

Just for me.

TWENTY-ONE

Declan

I drive slowly through Sycamore Falls, letting the glow of Christmas lights on all the houses fill the spaces I used to keep empty. Happy hour with Joshua went later than I expected. We talked more than we ever have. Laughed. Argued about football. He told me about his latest work project.

And I listened. *Really* listened. Like a father should.

Like I wanted *my* father to listen to me all those years ago, instead of constantly looking at me like I was a waste of space.

As if *I* should have been in that casket instead of my mother.

I push the thought aside, refusing to let my father

get under my skin. Instead, I focus on my time with Joshua. On the relationship I'm building with him, despite my absence in his life until now.

I make the turn onto my street, and my gaze snags on Claire's townhouse like it always does. Warm white lights drip along the eaves, and a glowing wreath hangs on her door. Even the little potted evergreen beside the steps is wrapped in gold ribbon.

A laugh slips out at the memory of her face when I told her I hadn't put up a tree in years.

I was so close to telling her why. How Christmas trees always remind me of my mom. How the idea of having a tree in my house has always been unbearable.

A symbol of my guilt.

My blame.

But now, as I pull into the driveway of my temporary home and glance toward the window where a modest tree glows through the glass, it doesn't hurt the way I thought it would. I expected a stab to the chest, an ache I'd carry all season.

Instead, warmth fills me.

This tree isn't a reminder of my past or the blame I've shouldered for years.

It's a reminder of Joshua. Of making new memories with him last weekend as we strung lights and hung ornaments.

And if I'm being honest, it's a reminder of Claire,

too. The way she put her apprehension aside and helped me pick out a tree when she saw how out of my element I was. The comfort I felt in a place that made me anxious seconds beforehand.

Killing the engine, I step into the chilly evening air, inhaling the aroma of pine that seems to permeate this town.

Then something slices through the quiet. A shrill, insistent beeping that detonates inside my skull. Smoke detector. Rapid. High. Relentless.

It shouldn't make my whole body fold in on itself. It shouldn't make my hands go cold and my vision narrow to a tiny, sharp pinprick.

It's not just a sound to me. It's a memory.

I can still smell the putrid smoke.

Can still feel the heat of the fire.

Can still hear the incessant beeping of the smoke detectors going off as our house was reduced to rubble.

And what makes the panic tighten around me like a noose is the realization that the beeping isn't coming from *my* townhouse.

It's coming from Claire's.

A full-body jolt hits me, and I sprint across the driveway and toward her front door, my pulse slamming against my ribs. Thankfully, there are no signs of smoke from the windows, but that doesn't mean anything. My childhood home was engulfed in flames in minutes.

I try the knob, but it's locked.

"Claire?" I shout, pounding on the door. No answer.

But her car's in the driveway.

I spin and run into my house, tearing through the kitchen and out onto the shared deck, rushing toward the sliding glass door. I pull on it, prepared to smash the glass if need be. Thankfully, it opens, and I rush inside.

No flames. No scorched walls. No blistering heat engulfing me.

Just Claire in the kitchen, totally oblivious to my presence. She's wearing oversized pink headphones that make her look absurdly cute, dancing and singing "All I Want for Christmas is You". She's searing something in a pan, smoke curling toward the ceiling as the alarm shrieks overhead.

I grab a chair and climb on it, my fingers fumbling around until the beeping stops. When it does, the silence rushes back in, feeling unnervingly loud.

Only then does Claire turn.

"Declan!" she gasps, ripping off her headphones. "What are you—"

"Your smoke detector was going off."

"Sorry." She laughs sheepishly, turning off the

burner and removing the cast iron skillet from the heat. "Our exhaust fan is broken so whenever I sear anything…." She gestures to the smoke. "This happens. I've learned to ignore it."

"Ignore it?" I stare at her, incredulous.

"I was in the mood for an ahi salad tonight." She gives me another sheepish smile, setting the tuna steak on a cutting board. "Sorry if it bothered you."

"Bothered me?"

The words come out ragged, uneven.

Before I can wrap my head around what I'm doing, I close the space between us in three strides, my still shaking hands framing her face.

Her eyes widen and her breath catches, but she doesn't pull away. As if she can sense I need this. Need to feel her skin against mine. Feel her warmth. Feel the reminder that she's here. That she's alive.

"I thought…" I shake my head, struggling to get the words out.

I'm still in that house, smoke so thick I can't breathe, my mother urging me to run.

"Thought what?" she asks softly, her eyes locked on mine. She reaches up and cups my cheek, her touch grounding me to the present instead of the past that still torments me every damn day.

Except with her.

With her, I can forget.

With her, I can breathe again.

"I was afraid I lost you, too," I admit.

Her brows knit, and she parts her lips. I sense she wants to ask what I mean.

She doesn't.

Instead, she rubs my cheek with her thumb, slow and reassuring, "I'm fine. I'm here."

I blow out a breath and press my forehead to hers, breathing her in. Warm vanilla from her body wash. The faint scent of white wine on her lips. The steady rhythm of her breath against mine.

"You're here," I echo.

She nods slowly. "I'm here."

I pull back slightly, just enough to drag my thumb over her bottom lip. She shivers, and it goes straight to my gut.

Her hands drift to my chest, and for a fleeting moment, I expect her to push against me. Put space between us.

She doesn't.

Instead, she clutches my shirt.

The smart thing, the *right* thing, would be to step back. But I'm not feeling smart right now. I'm feeling the weeks of restraint fraying with every heartbeat.

So I lean closer, the seconds stretching as I inch my lips toward her. Testing how far I can go.

And she still doesn't fight me, even when my lips are a whisper away from hers.

"Tell me to stop," I murmur, my voice low and

rough, almost begging her to put on the brakes since I'm not capable of doing it myself.

"I…"

"Claire." I meet her gaze, desperate for something. Permission. Damnation. At this point, I don't care. "Tell me to stop. Otherwise, I'm going to do what I've been wanting to do since I left you in Boston."

"What's that?"

"I think you know."

She inches her lips closer, the promise of her kiss within reach. "I wouldn't want to presume. So why don't you show me? Then I can decide if I want you to stop."

Goddamn this woman. She doesn't play fair. She never has. It's one of the things that drives me crazy about her.

"Show me, Declan," she encourages when I don't immediately make a move, her grip on my shirt tightening even more. "Show me what you've wanted to do since Boston."

I don't hesitate. Don't pause to think how wrong this is.

Instead, I do as she asks and crush my lips to hers.

TWENTY-TWO

Claire

Declan's lips are urgent, almost punishing, but I meet him with the same desperation.

Weeks of wanting, of staring too long, of pulling away before we crossed the point of no return ignite like gasoline meeting a flame. My fingers twist in the fabric of his shirt, yanking him closer until we're chest to chest, heat to heat.

But it's not close enough.

Every nerve in my body is tuned to him. The faint scrape of his stubble against my skin. The hard line of his chest pressed against mine. The deep, guttural sound in his throat that sends heat spiraling low in my belly.

I shouldn't be doing this. It would hurt Joshua if

he ever found out. He's been my friend for decades. Not to mention, he once asked me to marry him. Declan is his father, for crying out loud.

This isn't merely crossing a line.

It's setting fire to the line and dancing on the ashes.

But I can't seem to stop.

Not now that his lips are kissing mine, his tongue tangling with mine in a way that both exhilarates and frightens me.

Maybe this is what we both need. One night to get it out of our systems. Then things can go back to normal. He can go back to being Joshua's father. I can go back to being Joshua's best friend. And we can forget we were ever more than that.

Except I know better.

Because Declan isn't the kind of man you can easily forget.

The past several weeks are proof of that.

Declan tears his mouth from mine, his heavy pants echoing around us as he stares at me with an expression I can't quite label. Like he's caught between sin and salvation.

For a fleeting moment, I expect for him to come to his senses. Remind me why we can't do this.

Instead, he rasps, "When will Dylan be home?"

"I never know," I admit, still lightheaded from his

kiss. "Sometimes early. Sometimes late. Depends on the client."

He gives a curt nod. Then in one swift motion, he picks me up and hauls me over his shoulder like I weigh nothing, his arm firm around the back of my thighs.

"Declan!" I squeal through my laughter, my hair swinging toward the floor as the world turns upside down. "What the hell are you doing?"

"Taking you to my place," he replies without slowing. "That way, I don't have to worry about being interrupted. With what I have planned for you, I *really* don't want to be interrupted."

A sharp slap lands on my ass, and I squeal again, wriggling half-heartedly.

"You know I can walk," I admonish as he crosses the shared deck connecting our townhouses.

"If you can walk, you can run." He carries me inside his place, walking past the kitchen and down the hallway. "And I'm not letting you escape me. Not now that I finally have you."

He steps inside the bedroom and sets me on my feet. I lift my eyes to his, taking in his distinguished features illuminated in the soft glow of the bedside lamp.

For the first time since I learned who he is, I allow myself to *really* look at him. At the strong cut of his jaw. The faint groove between his brows. The heat in those blue eyes.

But it's not his features that undo me. It's the way he looks at me. Like I'm a treasure. Like I'm special. Like I matter.

"I don't think I could escape you, even if I wanted to," I tell him in a rare moment of honesty. "Believe me." I laugh under my breath. "I've tried."

He steps closer, pushing a tendril of hair behind my ear. "I've tried, too."

"It was only one night," I say like I have so many times before. But this time, I'm saying it in the hopes he'll have some sort of explanation for how I could feel this way about someone I barely know.

"We both know it was so much more than that."

I can't bring myself to argue. I just close my eyes and nod. "I know."

His lips find mine again, slower this time, almost reverent. The heat's still there, but now it's tempered with something heavier. Something that makes my knees weaken. That makes my heart swell. That makes my body warm.

He steers me toward the bed, stopping right before my legs hit the mattress.

"Do you know what I regret about Boston?" he murmurs, his mouth still hovering over mine.

"What's that?"

"That I didn't get to undress you myself. Don't get me wrong," he adds quickly. "I loved watching you strip for me." A wicked smile curves his mouth. "I've replayed that nightly while I got myself off."

"Is that right?" I tease.

"Among other memories from our night together." He winks. "But I swore if I ever got another chance with you, I wouldn't make the same mistake." He dips his head closer, feathering his lips along the curve of my neck. "I'd unwrap you myself."

"I'm not a gift," I manage, my breath hitching as his mouth finds the sensitive spot right below my ear.

He cups my cheeks in his hands, not allowing me to escape him. "To me, you are."

He claims my mouth again, treating me to a kiss that makes the rest of the world fall away. How did I go so long without this man's kiss? Without his touch? Without *him*?

Now that he's here, I don't want to waste another minute. We've already wasted enough time.

I pull out of the kiss and give him a flirtatious smile. "Well, what are you waiting for? You want to undress me?" With a challenge in my eyes, I take a small step back. "Undress me."

His gaze turns molten, raking over me, as if he's trying to decide where to start. Then he moves toward me, reaching for the hem of my t-shirt.

But he doesn't yank it over my head like I expected. He takes his time, his fingers skimming the skin above my hip bone as his lips brush my neck again, his teeth nibbling.

"Don't tell me you're the type to carefully unwrap every present without ripping the paper," I tease. "Christmas morning must have taken *forever* with you."

He pulls back slightly and something flickers in his eyes. Sadness. Regret, maybe. But just as quickly, his expression shifts, replaced by that teasing glint I know too well.

"Let me guess," he begins with a sly smile. "You rip into the wrapping without a second thought."

"Of course."

"What about the anticipation? The build up? If you unwrap all your gifts quickly, you'll have nothing left to look forward to."

"That's where you're wrong, Declan." I hoist myself onto my toes, my lips a breath from his.

"How so?"

"Because that's when the *real* fun begins. Once I've unwrapped all my presents, I get to *play* with them." I trail my hand down his chest, over the firm muscles of his stomach, then land on his crotch, cupping him through his dark jeans. "And Christmas presents deserve to be played with."

He sucks in a sharp breath and hardens beneath my palm. "Goddamn."

"Shall I give you a demonstration of how I like to play with my toys?"

He grips my face, his chest heaving. "Fuck, yes."

TWENTY-THREE

Declan

I help Claire shove my pants down, my fingers fumbling like they've forgotten how to work. My coat and shirt hit the floor in a careless heap, shoes kicked aside. Her hands are on me immediately, nails scraping down my chest, and then she's sinking to her knees like she's meant to be there.

And when she drags her tongue along her lips, I'm surprised I don't come right away.

I've always found Claire gorgeous. You'd have to be blind not to.

But right now? On her knees in front of me with her wide eyes trained on mine, her lips parted slightly as she wraps her hand around my throbbing dick?

She's never looked so damn irresistible.

The seconds seem to stretch as she slides her hand up and down my length, slow and methodical. As if she has all the time in the world.

As if she's not driving me crazy with every delicious pull.

Finally, she parts her lips even more and takes me in her mouth. I can't stop the sound that rips out of me. Low. Rough. Almost desperate. I tip my head back, squeezing my eyes shut as her tongue moves in slow, deliberate strokes, the kind that makes every muscle in my body lock tight.

I fist my hand in her hair, fighting the urge to hold her there and take control. It would be too easy to let go. To lose myself completely.

"You look so damn beautiful with your mouth full of cock."

She moans, increasing her motions.

"Your mouth full of *my* cock," I growl, my restraint slipping more and more with each tease of her tongue.

She closes her eyes and squirms, as if trying to dull the ache inside of her. I can only imagine how wet she is right now. What I wouldn't give to slide my fingers through her dripping cunt. To bury my face between her legs.

The mere thought makes me even harder, that familiar sensation forming low in my stomach. I can feel the edge looming. Can sense my control slipping.

So I step back before it's too late, my chest heaving.

She looks up, confused. "Did I do something wrong?"

I haul her up, my lips grazing her ear. "The opposite. You were doing everything right. But as much as I love fucking your mouth…" My hand drifts down, teasing her through the thin barrier of her shorts. "I need to fuck your cunt." I touch my forehead to hers, my voice dropping to a rasp. "Can I do that?"

"God, yes," she exhales.

"Then I guess it's my turn to unwrap a present."

She gives me a flirtatious grin. "I guess it is."

My lips find the slope of her neck, her pulse hammering beneath her skin, and I taste her. Warm. Sweet. Addictive.

"What are you doing?" she whines. "You're supposed to unwrap your present."

I smile against her, my fingers tracing idle circles over her hips. "I am. But unlike you, I like the anticipation of slowly unwrapping my gift. It makes the payoff even sweeter when I get to play with my new toy."

Her nails dig into me. "You're going to drive me crazy."

That's the idea. Watching her come undone like this is intoxicating. *Too* intoxicating. This is the part that's dangerous. The part where I forget every reason I should stop.

And it's not because of Joshua.

It's because of the way Claire makes me feel.

I've been with plenty of women in my forty-two years.

Not a single one ever made me feel like this. Like I'm unraveling, piece by piece.

And I don't know what to do about it.

I kiss her hard, pushing down the nagging feeling of doubt bubbling inside me. With my hand on her hip, I steer her toward the bed, tearing my lips from hers as I lay her down and settle between her legs.

"Time to play with my toy." I waggle my brows. "But I have a confession."

She tilts her head. "What's that?"

"I used to have a bad habit of putting my toys in my mouth first."

Her lips curve as she threads her fingers through my hair. "Is that right?"

I slowly nod. "It is."

"Then what are you waiting for?"

She places her hand on my shoulders, encouraging me to slide down her body. But just like when I undressed her, I take my time, relishing the feel of her soft skin.

I pull a nipple between my lips, circling my tongue, then bite softly. She moans, her nails digging harder into my scalp. But she doesn't ask me to stop. Doesn't ask me to hurry. She stays in the moment with me.

I move to her other breast, giving it the same treatment before snaking down her frame, tasting every single inch of skin. As I do, Claire grows even more needy, her hips circling in desperation, her chest heaving through her ragged breaths.

God, I love watching her unravel like this. Love seeing how much I turn her on. Love how damn responsive she is.

I've never been with another woman like her. Sure, the others did all the right things. Moaned when I touched them. Cried out when I fucked them.

But it was never like this. Never felt like they were on the brink of combusting from just my touch.

And I never felt this sort of raw desperation like I do with Claire.

When I reach her waist, I hesitate, lifting my eyes to meet hers. They're fiery, full of hunger and want and need.

And I love that I do this to her.

"Go on, Declan," she encourages as she slides a hand down her stomach and begins to rub her clit. "Put your toy in your mouth."

I groan, pushing her thighs farther apart. For several seconds, I watch as Claire touches herself. It's killing me not to taste her. Not to bury my face in her cunt, but I love watching her do this, too. Love seeing how comfortable she is with me now, especially after how nervous she was doing this in front of me mere weeks ago.

"Tell me, Claire," I rasp out, licking my lips as my tongue salivates with the promise of her taste.

"Yes, Declan," she moans.

"Whenever you've touched yourself over the past few weeks, did you think of me?"

"God, yes."

"What were you thinking about?"

"Everything." She rubs herself faster, and I press a hand to her wrist, preventing her from touching herself.

"Tell me," I admonish. "Tell me exactly what you were thinking."

"How incredible it felt when you fucked me. How you gave me what I needed. How you didn't judge me for wanting you to spank me or bite me or pull my hair."

I move up her body, cupping her cheeks. "I would *never* judge you for sharing your desires. There's nothing wrong with liking what you do." I give her a slight smile. "And it just so happens I like the same things."

I press my lips back to hers, our tongues touching briefly before I pull away and settle back between her legs, pushing her thighs even wider.

"Now, I want you to come on my tongue, Claire."

I slide my tongue up her center before wrapping my lips around her clit and sucking. I can't help the groan that escapes from the taste of her. It's like I've been starving without even knowing it. Every sound she makes vibrates through me, each one pulling me deeper under.

I give her what she likes, what she needs, sucking and nibbling on her clit as I push a finger inside her, then another. It doesn't take long for her body to tense. She grips my hair, as if needing something to keep her grounded, fighting the inevitable. But it's a losing battle. The last few weeks have taught me that.

"Come on, Claire." I increase my motions, thrusting my fingers in and out of her with even more urgency. "Don't fight it, baby. Come for me. Now."

I give her pussy a light slap, and it's like a hairpin trigger, her body spasming around me as she cries out my name. I should savor this, but I don't. I need to be inside her. Now.

I climb back over her, bringing my erection up to her entrance. Then I thrust into her, her walls clenching around me like they never want to let me go. My hands cradle her face, our ragged breaths crashing in the space between us.

"How does my toy like to be played with?" My voice is low, uneven. "Should I take it easy? Or test her limits?"

Her nails rake down my back, and she catches my earlobe between her teeth. "Test her limits."

"I was hoping you'd say that."

I hook her legs over my shoulders and drive into her harder. Each thrust is brutal, deliberate. Nothing soft. Nothing tender. I tell myself it's safer this way. If I treat her like every other woman, maybe she won't be any different.

But I know it's a lie.

I could tell Claire was different before I ever touched her. Before I felt her. Before I tasted her.

It's why I haven't been able to stay away.

Why I know it's going to kill me when I have to.

Because there's no future here.

She deserves more than I'm capable of giving her.

I just have to keep reminding myself of that.

TWENTY-FOUR

Claire

The steady thrum of Declan's heartbeat soothes me as I rest on his chest, his arm draped around me like he's never letting go. Neither of us moves. Neither of us wants to. Instead, we both seem content to stay right here, in this moment.

I'm still trying to wrap my head around the fact that I'm here at all.

When Parker essentially forced me to go home and take a night off, I'd planned to make dinner and binge reality TV as I sipped on a glass of wine. I never could have anticipated I'd end up in bed with Declan.

I can't stop replaying the look on his face when he came bursting into my townhouse. The terror in his eyes as he clutched my cheeks. The tremble in his hands. The crack in his voice when he said he was scared he'd lost me, too.

It could be nothing, but I can't shake the feeling there's a deeper meaning to his words.

Who else did he lose?

My stomach interrupts my thoughts with a loud growl, making me cringe.

Declan's arm tightens around me, and he presses a soft kiss to my head that makes me feel things I have no business feeling.

"Hungry?" he murmurs, his voice low and rough.

"Someone did interrupt my dinner plans so he could put his cock in me," I deadpan.

"I didn't hear you complaining." He rolls to face me, grabbing my thigh and hooking my leg over his hip. "In fact, if memory serves, you said 'Oh, yes, Declan.'" He pitches his voice higher in a horrible impersonation of me. "'Harder. You fuck me so good. You must have a magical penis.'"

I playfully pinch his side. "I did not say you had a magical penis."

He circles against me, his erection hitting that spot I'm desperate to feel him again. "Maybe not out loud. But you thought it. Didn't you?"

I bite my bottom lip, fighting back my moan. "Maybe."

"Good. Because I kept thinking about how

fucking magical your pussy is." He slides his finger between us and gently rubs my clit as he catches my mouth in a kiss.

But then my treacherous stomach growls again.

He breaks away with a chuckle. "Time to feed you."

"Your magical penis?"

He rolls away and stands up from the bed. "No. *Actual* food." He grabs his boxer briefs and tugs them on. "You need your strength for what I have planned for you later."

"You don't need to go to the trouble. I can just go back home."

I start to get up, but he pushes me back onto the bed, crawling on top of me and pinning me down.

"Not a chance in hell. I'm not done with you yet, Claire."

His mouth captures mine in another heated kiss, and I melt into him.

My brain shouts at me to leave. Put some distance between us before this turns into something I can't control. But I don't. Because thinking clearly around Declan is impossible.

"Dinner will be ready in about thirty minutes. Feel free to use the shower if you'd like."

He leaves me with one last kiss on my forehead, then disappears down the hall. I reluctantly get out of Declan's bed and pad into the bathroom.

The faint scent of his cologne clings to the air, grounding and disarming all at once. His toiletries line the marble counter — toothpaste, mouthwash, shaving cream. It's not cluttered like my vanity. Another stark reminder of how different we are. He's all precision and organization. I'm chaos and creativity.

I head toward the shower and turn on the water. Once it's the right temperature, I pin up my hair and step under the stream, sighing as the water hits me.

Even though I'm not washing my hair, I reach for his shampoo and open the cap, inhaling. It smells like him. Masculine, earthy, with some clean undertones that make me want to drown myself in his scent.

After a longer shower than necessary, considering I didn't wash my hair, I wrap myself in an oversized towel and return to the bedroom. I'm about to put my clothes back on, but spot Declan's button-down shirt on the floor. Grinning to myself, I pick it up and slip it on, fastening only the lower few buttons.

When I step into the kitchen, Declan glances up from the cutting board, then does a double take, heat building in his stare as he sets down the knife.

"On second thought," he begins, his voice low as he stalks toward me, "maybe I'll just have *you* for dinner." He wraps an arm around me and yanks me against him.

"You won't hear any complaints from me."

He kisses me, but my stomach interrupts again.

I can feel his smile against my lips. "But I'd be a terrible host if I let you go hungry." He touches a soft kiss to my mouth, then pulls back, returning to the cutting board. "This won't take long. I wasn't sure what you'd like so I went with salmon since that's what you ordered at dinner with Joshua."

"You remember?"

He meets my gaze. "I remember everything about you."

A tiny breath escapes at the sincerity in his voice, and I quickly look away, not wanting to get swept up in it. It doesn't mean anything. Doesn't change the fact that this will never go anywhere.

Instead, I take in my surroundings. I haven't been in this townhouse since Finn moved out. Despite the furniture being mostly the same, it feels different.

The tree I helped Declan pick out sits decorated by the front window. Other than that, there's nothing of a personal nature. Even the countertops are free of clutter. Unlike my kitchen, which is often overflowing with all of Dylan's cookware and spices.

At the thought, I'm instantly reminded of the mess I left behind.

"I should go clean up before Dylan gets home. I'd hate for her to—"

"Already done."

I blink. "What?"

"I went over while you were in the shower. Don't worry. I checked the driveway first to make sure her car wasn't there. I put your tuna in a container and cleaned up everything else. Our secret's safe."

He gives me a sly wink, and I'm not sure how to feel about being his secret. Hearing it out loud hits me harder than I expected, leaving me momentarily ashamed.

"Would you like some wine?" Declan asks, cutting through my unease.

"Sure."

He pours two glasses of chardonnay and hands me one.

"Cheers."

I clink my glass with his. "Cheers."

When he turns toward the stove, I hoist myself onto a barstool by the kitchen island and watch him sear the salmon, my eyes drawn to the lines of his shoulders, the way his jaw flexes as he concentrates.

I've always found him to be attractive. But watching him cook?

This may be the sexiest thing I've ever seen, especially since he's only wearing boxer briefs.

"What are you thinking about over there?" He meets my gaze.

"You may have just unlocked a new kink."

"A new kink?" He arches a brow.

"Yeah. You cooking in just your boxer briefs. It's a definite turn-on."

His laughter fills the space, the sound sending a rush of excitement through me. "Well, just wait until dessert."

"You're making dessert, too?"

He turns off the burner and glances my way, his eyes filled with lust. "I don't need to."

A shiver rolls down my spine, and I squeeze my legs together to dull the ache building inside. How does this man seem to turn me on with just one look? One word?

"Hope you like it." He sets a plate in front of me before sliding onto the barstool beside me.

"It looks delicious."

I slice into the salmon, having to bite back a moan from the buttery flavor. One thing is certain. Declan can cook. I'm not sure why I'm so surprised by this. I guess I had this image in my head of him hiring someone like Dylan to prepare all his meals. Or ordering takeout, considering all the hours he works.

"Is it okay?" he asks, his expression somewhat pinched and nervous.

"It's fantastic. Thanks for going to the trouble. You didn't have to."

"It's the least I can do after I interrupted your dinner plans."

"I'm sorry about before." I wave my hand. "The smoke detector. I didn't mean to disturb you."

"I told you. You didn't disturb me, Claire. You *scared* me." He holds my gaze for several long beats before refocusing his attention on his salmon.

I should drop it, but I can't get his words from earlier out of my head. How he thought he lost me, too.

It's the *too* that won't leave me alone.

"What you said before… How you were afraid you lost me, too. What did you mean?"

His back goes rigid, and he stares ahead, the room going eerily silent. I swear I can hear my own heartbeat in the stillness, even the dog barking down the street going mute.

"I'm sorry," I say after several awkward seconds. "I didn't mean to pry. It's not my place." I avert my gaze as another silence settles between us, this one even heavier than before.

I'm about to push back from my chair and make up an excuse about needing to get home when his voice cuts through.

"My mother."

"What about your mother?" I ask cautiously.

From the bits and pieces he's shared over the past few weeks, I had a feeling she'd passed when he was young, but I never pressed for more information. It wasn't my place.

Now I can't help but be curious.

"I lost her, too." His eyes finally meet mine. "In a house fire. *Our* house."

I suck in a sharp breath. "Oh, god."

I wasn't sure what I expected him to say. Maybe a car accident. Or cancer. But a fire? I can't imagine what that must have been like. The helplessness as you watch your entire life go up in flames? It's one of my biggest fears.

"It was Christmas Eve," he continues softly. "I was eight and was at that age where I was questioning whether Santa was real. I decided I was going to prove it one way or another that year, so I tried to stay awake, listening for anything that might sound like reindeer and a sleigh."

A nostalgic smile tugs on his mouth as he looks into the distance, as if watching a movie of his childhood play before his eyes. But then his expression falls.

"At some point, I dozed off. The next thing I knew, my mom barged into my room and woke me up. I was disoriented. Had trouble focusing. It took me a few seconds to realize why. There was smoke everywhere. She told me I needed to get out of the house. But in that moment of panic, all I could think about was our cat." He laughs under his breath. "He was a complete asshole. Hated everyone except me, considering I was the one who found him in a bush by our bus stop.

Regardless, she promised to find him, then told me to grab my brother and get out of the house."

I'm almost afraid to ask. "What happened next?"

"I did as she asked. Ran into my brother's room and got him out safely."

"And your mom?"

"After what felt like an eternity, she stumbled out with the cat." He swallows hard. "She handed him to me, then collapsed. The smoke… It was too much for her lungs to handle, and she died on the way to the hospital."

I squeeze my eyes shut, seeing Declan in a completely different light. Seeing his *actions* in a completely different light. No wonder he overreacted when he heard my smoke detector going off. It must have brought back some horrific memories.

"And your father?" I ask after several long moments. "Where was he when all of this happened?"

"Out buying batteries so we'd be able to play with our presents when we opened them."

"Sounds like a good man."

"At one point he was."

"What do you mean?"

"After that night…he wasn't the same. He couldn't stand Christmas." His jaw tightens. "Or me."

I furrow my brow. "Why?"

"He blamed me for what happened and had no problem letting me know it. He wasn't wrong. It *is* my fault my mother died. If I hadn't begged her to find the cat—"

"You can't seriously blame yourself for her death," I retort, my voice heavy with disbelief.

"Why wouldn't I?"

"Because it wasn't your fault."

He blows out a disbelieving laugh as he takes a large gulp of wine. "It's a sweet sentiment, Claire, but you're wrong. I've learned to live with it."

Now I'm the one to push out a disbelieving laugh, because it's obvious he hasn't. He's just learned to bury it beneath the surface.

"Your mother made a choice. If I were in her shoes and my son asked me to save his cat, I probably would have done the same thing. As for your father, I take back what I said. He sounds like a fucking asshole."

"Maybe, but he has a point. It was—"

"I told you how my father left my mother when she was pregnant with me," I interject before he can blame himself yet again.

"You did."

"A part of me has always thought that maybe if my mother wasn't pregnant with me, he would have stayed. But anytime I even suggested it, my mother shot me down. Insisted I wasn't to blame. Like a good parent should."

He stares at me for a protracted beat, then sighs, shifting his eyes forward as he pushes his salad around his plate. "I appreciate your words, Claire, but our situations are a little different."

"If you ask me, they're not that different at all. You lost your mother. I lost my father. But my mother refused to let me blame myself, whereas your father was more than happy to let you shoulder the blame." I shake my head in disgust. "That's not what a real parent would do, even if you *were* at fault, which you're not."

He parts his lips to protest yet again, but I raise a hand, cutting him off.

"You have a son. Would you ever treat him the way your father did? If you were in your father's shoes, would you blame Joshua?"

"God, no," he answers quickly. "I'd never do that."

"Exactly." I fully face him and grab his hands in mine. "You weren't to blame, Declan. You *aren't* to blame. What happened to your mother was tragic, and I hate that you had to learn that kind of suffering at such a young age. But I hate what your father made you endure more. Because he was wrong. And cruel. You didn't deserve that. You didn't—"

Before I can utter another syllable, he crushes his lips to mine in a kiss that completely steals my breath. This one feels different from all the other times he's kissed me. I'm not sure how to explain it. This one isn't filled with lust or hunger, although there's still a spark of electricity buzzing between us. This one feels more emotional. More sensual. More…personal.

Which is everything this isn't supposed to be.

When he finally pulls back, he rests his forehead against mine. "How are you so damn wise and only twenty-four?"

"I'm an old soul."

"I know. It's what drew me to you that night in the bar."

"And here I thought it was my legs," I tease, hoping to cut through the mounting tension. "Or my incredible rack."

"Oh, I definitely like both of those," he says with a devilish glint in his eye. "But I like what's behind that incredible rack more."

He curves toward me and captures my mouth in another kiss, this one even more tender than before.

Even more emotional.

I should stop this. Thank him for the orgasms and dinner, then escape to the safety of my home.

Instead, I allow myself to sink further into the fantasy that we could be more than this.

That this could be real.
That this could be forever.
Even though I know it can't.

TWENTY-FIVE

Declan

Claire's body is molded against mine, her head tucked under my chin, the steady rhythm of her breathing warm against my chest. My arm is draped over her, my hand resting on the curve of her hip. I can feel every subtle rise and fall, every quiet shift of muscle beneath her skin. She feels like she belongs here. Like she's *always* belonged here.

And I don't know what the hell to make of it.

The room is dim with only the faintest wash of a streetlight filtering through the blinds, striping her bare shoulder in gold. The air still smells of her, warm vanilla tangled with something sharper and more intoxicating. Eucalyptus maybe.

My pulse hasn't quite slowed, but it's not just the

memory of her body clenching around me, my name on her lips as she came undone.

It's *her*. All of her. Being with her makes me act like someone I don't recognize.

Like when I told her about my past.

I've never shared that story with anyone. Not the ugly, raw truth about my mother's death and the way my father looked at me afterward. I usually keep it short. Tell people I lost my mother when I was young and let them fill in the blanks however they want. But with Claire… I wanted her to know. *Needed* her to know.

And that scares the hell out of me.

Her phone chimes, sharp and intrusive against the quiet. She shifts in my arms, and for a selfish second I consider holding her tighter, keeping her pinned to me so she can't move. But she slips free and rolls over, grabbing her cell off the nightstand, a groan escaping her.

"Everything okay?" I ask, my voice low.

"It's Dylan. She's on her way home. I should probably go."

"You don't have to. You could—"

"We both know I do." Her eyes soften with something like hope, but her tone is firm.

"Yeah," I agree, albeit reluctantly. "You're right."

She slides out of bed, the sheets dragging over my skin as she leaves, taking her heat with her. I watch her in silence as she moves around the room, collecting her clothes and pulling them on.

It's not the first time I've shared my bed with someone and watched them leave afterward. Usually, I'm fine with it. Hell, I *prefer* it. No messy attachments. No lingering. No promises I have no intention of keeping.

But this feels wrong. Like there's something unfinished between us.

"Maybe we can—"

"It's okay." She cuts me off before I can finish whatever I was going to say. What that is, I'm not quite sure.

"What do you mean?" I frown.

"Whatever you were about to say… It's okay." She pulls her t-shirt over her head and meets my gaze. "I knew what this was when I got into bed with you, Declan. We're both consenting adults, and tonight was incredible. But there's no need to turn this into something it's not and can never be."

I know she's right. Know this can never become anything more than it already is. Hell, tonight shouldn't have happened in the first place. The best thing I can do right now is let her go.

But when she turns from me and starts toward the door, that's easier said than done. I'm up and across the room in two long strides, catching her wrist and tugging her against me.

Her breath hitches, green eyes locking on mine, full of questions I don't have answers to. I have no idea what I'm doing. But I do know one thing.

I can't let her leave without one more taste.

I crash my mouth down on hers, hard and unrestrained. There's too much I want to tell her. Too much I shouldn't. So I let the kiss say it all instead. The craving. The frustration. The dangerous pull between us neither of us can seem to fight but know we need to.

I tear myself away before I lose the last of my restraint, breathing hard. My hand lingers against her jaw for one more second, memorizing the shape of her face beneath my palm. Then I step back, releasing her from my hold.

She turns to leave again. This time, I let her, watching as she disappears down the hallway.

When I hear the sliding door close, the entire townhouse feels colder.

TWENTY-SIX

Claire

I'm late.

Not by much, but enough to put me in power-walk mode down the icy sidewalk of Main Street, my boots clicking in a staccato rush, my scarf hanging half-wrapped because I couldn't be bothered to loop it properly.

Normally, I'm up before my alarm goes off. Today, I hit snooze. Twice. It felt like I'd only just closed my eyes when that stupid chime went off.

I can't remember the last time I slept that well.

Actually, that's not entirely true. I can.

Boston. After the night I spent with Declan.

I fight against a smile, but it still tugs at my lips

anyway. It must be the effect of his magical penis, as he so eloquently put it. And God help me, he's not wrong. The things he made me feel… I didn't think I'd ever experience them again.

I'm so lost in my thoughts of last night that I'm barely paying attention where I'm going. So much so that I don't notice the slick patch of ice on the side-walk until it's too late.

The world tilts, and I reach for something to prevent me from falling, but there's nothing to grab on to. I brace myself to hit the sidewalk.

But it never comes.

Instead, a pair of strong hands clamp around my hips, yanking me back against a solid chest. My breath whooshes from my lungs, and a familiar scent hits me. Citrus. Wood. Spice.

I dart my head up, and Declan's eyes lock on mine, a faint smile curving his mouth.

"Hey." His voice is low, rough, and far too sensual for eight in the morning.

"Hey." My reply comes out breathy.

"Hey," he repeats, softer this time. Like he's testing how it feels between us.

"Hey," I say again, too transfixed by the feel of his hands on my body to come up with a single coherent thought.

I should step back. Put distance between us. But

my body isn't interested in logic. It's greedy for his touch. For the steady weight of his fingers splayed at my hips. He doesn't appear to be in any hurry to let go, either, his gaze tracing over my face, pausing on my lips in a way that makes my stomach flip.

I dart my tongue out to moisten them, and I swear his grip on me tightens.

But before the moment veers off into dangerous territory, a baby starts wailing somewhere down the block, breaking the spell. I push out of his hold, smoothing a tendril of hair behind my ear.

"Thanks," I say, trying for casual. "If you hadn't caught me, my ass would be all black and blue."

"You mean even *more* black and blue?" he murmurs.

Heat blooms low in my belly, vivid flashes of how ravenous he was for me after dinner last night flickering through my mind. His teeth clamped on my neck. His bruising grip on my hips. The sharp crack of his palm against my ass.

He'd warned me I'd need my energy for what he'd had planned.

He wasn't wrong.

The things he did. The things he made me feel. The pleasure I experienced.

And by the heat in his gaze, I know he's thinking about the same thing.

"Well… Thanks again," I manage, turning from him and continuing toward Bean & Bloom.

"Going to get coffee?" he asks, falling into step beside me.

"I am."

"I'll walk with you. I'm headed there, too."

Part of me wants to say no, too worried what people might think. But it's not like we planned this. We're just two people headed to the same place walking together. Nothing wrong with that. Or so I tell my guilty conscience.

The wind nips at my cheeks as we walk through downtown Sycamore Falls. Garland twists around every lamppost, strings of lights still twinkling faintly against the pale morning sky.

"It's beautiful," Declan says, glancing around. "Like something straight out of a Christmas card. You're lucky you grew up somewhere like this."

"Small towns have their disadvantages," I admit, "but I don't know if I'd want to live anywhere else. Unless I inherited a tropical island." I slow my steps as we approach the coffee shop. "Then I'd be on the first flight out."

He chuckles, holding the door for me.

Inside, the scent of espresso wraps around us. I smile at a few familiar faces but keep moving toward the counter.

"So is that your dream?" Declan asks as we join the line. "Moving to a tropical island?"

"More of a fantasy. I'd miss my mom and sister too much. Plus, I'm about to become an aunt."

"Congratulations."

"Thanks. What about you? Where would *you* live if you could go anywhere?"

He shrugs. "I like where I—"

"And you can't say where you live now," I cut in. "Anywhere *else* in the world. Where would you choose?"

His eyes find mine. "This place is growing on me. Especially the people. Especially *one* person in particular."

I swallow. That's the kind of thing people say when they're in a relationship. When they have feelings for each other. We're just two people who happen to have amazing sex.

Nothing more.

But before I can remind him of this, an annoyed voice calls my name. I tear my gaze from Declan to see the line in front of us has disappeared. I give the barista, Tilly, an apologetic smile and hurry up to the counter.

"A ginger tea and an Americano with steamed milk."

"Make that two Americanos," Declan says from

behind me, leaning in and handing Tilly a twenty, his body brushing against mine.

"You don't have to pay for my coffee. Or my sister's tea."

"'Tis the season of giving," he says with a mischievous grin. "And I really like giving."

Tilly looks from me to Declan, and I can see her brain spinning, which is never a good thing. I've known her most of my life. She was voted biggest gossip of our high school graduating class, which is saying something, considering we live in a small town full of gossips. The last thing I need is for Tilly to spread baseless rumors about seeing me and Joshua's dad getting all cozy at the coffee shop.

"Thanks."

As Tilly counts out his change, I move to the far end of the counter to put some space between us. I keep my eyes fixed on the baristas preparing espresso and steaming milk, as if it's the most fascinating thing I've ever seen. Anything to help me ignore the fluttering in my stomach, especially when I sense Declan approach from behind, the tiny hairs all over my body standing on end.

"I haven't been able to stop thinking about you," he murmurs after several seconds, his voice low, almost a growl. "Doesn't help that my bed still smells like you. And not just your body wash, either. It still smells like your cunt."

I close my eyes. "Declan…"

"I know." His breath is warm against my ear. "I know I shouldn't think about you like this. It's wrong on so many levels. Part of me thought last night would be enough. That I could get you out of my system."

"And did you?"

He huffs a laugh. "We both know the answer to that. We both know it's impossible."

I turn, meeting his gaze. "But this—"

"Can't go anywhere." He curves toward me. "But that doesn't make me want you any less. Doesn't make—"

"Declan!" the barista calls out. "Two Americanos and a ginger tea."

I quickly turn away, grateful for the welcome distraction, and approach the counter. I hand Declan his Americano before grabbing my two drinks, then start for the door.

I only make it a few steps before a hand on my forearm stops me.

"Have lunch with me today," Declan says, a cross between a request and a demand.

"What?"

"You get a lunch break, don't you?"

"I usually eat in my office while I work."

"But you *can* leave, right?"

"I suppose…" I draw out.

"Then spend it with me. I can meet you somewhere."

"How will you explain that to Joshua? This is a small town. He'll find out we had lunch together. People talk. They're probably already talking."

I look around the coffee shop. Tilly still glances our way every few seconds between taking orders, her expression a mixture of curiosity and suspicion.

"It's just lunch."

"That won't matter. Not around here."

"Fine. Then you can come to my place. I'll leave the back door unlocked so you won't be seen walking up to my front door. It'll look like you went home for lunch. No one will know."

I chew on my bottom lip. "I don't know, Declan."

It was one thing to sleep with him last night. But to keep sleeping together? I'm not sure I'm made for casual sex.

Then again, I had no problem having casual sex with Joshua.

That was different, though. There was no spark. No unrelenting craving I didn't think I'd ever be able to satisfy. Not like there is whenever I'm with Declan. He doesn't even need to touch me to cause this sort of visceral reaction. One look, and I'm putty in his very large, very capable hands.

"Just think about it," he suggests. "If you decide you'd rather spend lunch with a sad sandwich and your laptop, I'll understand." He leans closer, dropping his voice so I can barely hear him. "But if you'd rather spend an hour of your day with my face buried between your thighs, I'll be waiting." He pulls back, a devilish glint in his eyes once more. "Okay?"

I part my lips, about to berate him for not playing fair when another familiar voice interjects.

"Why am I not surprised to see you here?"

I jerk back as Joshua approaches. I attempt to move away from Declan, but there's nowhere to go in the crush of people. Joshua leans in and kisses my cheek before noticing Declan.

"I didn't realize you'd be here." They give each other a quick hug.

"You keep saying this place has the best coffee around." Declan lifts his cup. "I figured it was time to give it a try."

"You won't regret it." Joshua beams, looking between Declan and me. I bring my coffee to my lips, praying he didn't see or hear anything he wasn't supposed to.

"Did you two come together?" he asks, gesturing between us.

Heat floods my face at the double entendre, and it takes everything I have not to choke on my coffee.

"Just a happy coincidence," Declan answers smoothly.

"I need to run," I say quickly. "I have to drop

Gen's tea off at the library before heading to the ridge."

"See you there," Joshua says, and I manage a smile before slipping out the door.

That was close. *Too* close. All the more reason going over Declan's for lunch is a horrible idea.

But when I steal a glance over my shoulder and meet his eyes, I fear I won't be able to stay away.

TWENTY-SEVEN

Declan

The clock ticks louder than it has any right to, like a hammer striking steel in an empty room. Each second ricochets inside my skull, drowning out everything else.

I check the time yet again.

12:42.

I don't know what time Claire normally takes her lunch. Could be noon. Could be one. Then again, she did say she usually eats at her desk whenever she gets hungry.

Like I do.

But with every minute that passes, the more impatient I get.

I told her I wouldn't pressure her. That the choice was hers.

I just wish I knew what that choice was.

Steam curls from the pot on the stove, carrying the scent of roasted tomatoes and basil. I grab a wooden spoon and stir the soup. Once. Twice. Maybe twelve times. I don't know. All I know is the anticipation is killing me.

A car engine hums in the distance, tires crunching against snow and gravel. My heart skyrockets, and I dart toward the front window. But it's not her car. Heaving a sigh, I let the curtain fall back into place, trying not to be disappointed.

It's probably better if she doesn't come for lunch.

Safer.

But a reckless part of me wants her to walk through that door.

Wants her to choose me.

With slow steps, I trudge back across the living room. But I'll drive myself crazy if I don't do something to take my mind off Claire. So instead of stirring the soup for the umpteenth time, I head to the desk and open my laptop, pulling up one of the pleadings I should be working on.

Sentences line the screen, words that made complete sense when I wrote them. But now they have no meaning, my thoughts constantly drifting to Claire.

Her mouth against mine.

The silken feel of her hair in my fist.

The soft, captivating sound that breaks from her whenever she lets go.

The memory is so vivid.

So dangerous.

I squeeze my eyes shut and take a deep breath, hoping it will help me focus. Then the sound of a door opening cuts through.

I'm on my feet in seconds, trying not to get my hopes up. It could just be my imagination making me hear things.

Then Claire steps into the living area. Her cheeks are pink from the cold, but she's never looked so damn beautiful.

Because she's here.

"You came," I say roughly, partly surprised. Partly relieved.

"Not yet." She gives me a wicked smile and saunters toward me. "But I'm sure it's only a matter of time until I do." Her breath dances on my lips as she hoists herself onto her toes.

"You've got that right," I growl, dragging her flush against me and claiming her mouth.

Her lips are warm, insistent, tasting faintly of cinnamon. She melts into me, her body curving into mine like she's always belonged here. With my hand on her hip, I steer us toward the bedroom, even as my brain screams restraint.

She slides her hands under my shirt, her nails digging into my skin like she owns me.

She damn well might.

I've never experienced this before. Never begged for scraps of a woman's time. Never thought about her with every breath. Never craved her touch so badly I ache when she's gone.

And still, I can't stop myself.

"I thought we'd be having lunch," she teases, her words a husky murmur against my mouth as I fumble with the zipper of her jeans.

"We will," I rasp, trailing my lips down the elegant line of her jaw to the pulse fluttering at her throat. "But I want my dessert first."

She laughs, low and throaty. "Naughty boy."

"You're about to find out just how naughty I am."

I make quick work of ridding her of her clothes before throwing her onto my bed. I'm between her legs in mere seconds, treating myself to what I've been craving since last night.

The first taste of her cunt undoes me. It's hunger and reverence, desperation and devotion tangled in one. Every moan she gives me feeds the storm inside until I don't know where need ends and ruin begins.

And that's the truth. This woman could absolutely ruin me. Could destroy everything I'm trying to build.

But I meant what I told her this morning. That despite the ramifications, I can't seem to listen to reason when I'm around her.

I just hope it doesn't come back to bite me in the ass later.

TWENTY-EIGHT

Declan

The streets of Sycamore Falls are unrecognizable from when I first arrived.

Holiday music drifts from hidden speakers, threading itself through the chatter of the crowd. The scent of kettle corn and roasted chestnuts filters through, mingling with crisp, clean air. Red and green coats, scarves, and knit hats blur into one living stream of color, the sidewalks packed tight with tourists and locals waiting for the annual Christmas parade.

It makes me think of Claire.

These days, everything does.

She's spent every lunch break with me this past

week. Not that we've been eating. At least, not food. It's been the highlight of my day.

Maybe of the entire year.

It shouldn't be. My sole purpose in staying was to form a relationship with my son.

Not sneak around behind his back and fuck his best friend.

But I can't help myself.

The second she steps inside my townhouse, the world falls away. She's not the woman my son once asked to marry. And I'm not the man she can never have.

It's just her, me, and this intense connection I still can't explain.

"Sorry it's a bit of a walk." Joshua's voice yanks me back to the present. "It's easier to park at Holley Ridge than try to find a spot downtown."

I glance over the sea of people standing shoulder to shoulder along the curb. "I can see why. Quite the turnout."

"Sycamore Falls loves Christmas. People put out their chairs the night before to save their spot."

"They don't get stolen?"

Joshua laughs. "This is a small town. It's not like D.C."

I huff a dry sound. "You've got that right."

The city has always been my sanctuary. Its pace.

Its convenience. Its anonymity. There, I'm just another face. Invisible. Forgettable.

That's not the case here. People know who I am. They *see* me. They stop to talk to me. Are genuinely interested in how I'm liking my time here in town.

And it doesn't feel as suffocating as I thought it would. The place has grown on me.

Or, more accurately, one woman in particular has grown on me.

"Did you watch the parade when you were little?" I ask.

"We did. I looked forward to it every year." He peers into the distance, a nostalgic gleam crossing his expression. "Afterward, Mom would take me to see Santa at the hardware store, and I'd tell him what I wanted for Christmas. She always made sure I got it, too." He beams, then his smile falters, shadows flickering across his features. "I'm sorry. I always seem to bring her up. Don't I?"

"Joshua…" I slow my steps so he meets my eyes. "It's okay. Talk about her whenever you want. I didn't know her that well. Or at all, really. I was young and made more bad decisions than good. But I don't want you to feel like you can't talk about her around me."

He gives me a smile that looks so much like my own it jars me. "Thanks."

We wind through the crowd until he veers down a narrow side alley.

"Where are we going?" I ask, confused. "I thought we were watching the parade."

"We are," he says over his shoulder, his mouth curving into a sly grin. "From a much better spot."

I follow him toward a door in the back of a brick building, where he inputs a code and leads me up several flights of stairs before emerging onto a rooftop. But it's not a normal rooftop.

It's strung with white lights, warm against the picture-perfect blue sky. Patio furniture and high-tops are scattered across the terrace, long tables with *hors d'oeuvres* placed along the walls. A bar glows in the corner, golden light spilling over bottles of wine and beer. The air is alive with laughter, clinking glasses, and the crisp scent of spiced apple and pine.

"Where are we?" I ask as I take in my surroundings.

"The Wicked Hop," Joshua answers. "You remember Dylan, who lives next door to you?"

I nod.

"One of her older brothers, Jude, owns it. Every year, he invites close friends and family to watch the parade from up here. Food, drinks, best view in town. I hope this is okay," he adds quickly. "If you'd rather watch from down below, we can. I just thought—"

"This is definitely better than being in the crowd," I respond. "I don't think I'd like the parade as much if I had to stand down there."

"Me, neither."

He takes me around, introducing me to faces and names that clearly mean something to him. Friends who've become family. People who anchor him here in a way I've never been anchored anywhere.

But all I can think of is Claire.

If she'll be here, too.

After all, everyone Joshua has introduced me to has asked about her.

And her roommate, Dylan, is already here.

Maybe she's working. If she planned on being here, wouldn't she have come with Dylan? Wouldn't Joshua have said something?

Or am I just overthinking it, as always?

I do my best to push down all thoughts of Claire as Joshua introduces me to Dylan's older brother, Hayden, who seems to be about my age. But as I shake his hand, I feel that same prickle of awareness I do whenever Claire's around.

I steal a glance toward the door, not surprised to see her making her way along the rooftop terrace, two women at her side.

One is pregnant, with the same smile I've seen soften Claire's entire face. The other is older, silver-haired, with the same eyes that bewitched me from the moment I first saw them. I don't have to ask to know they're her sister and mother.

"There you are," Joshua says upon noticing her.

But her eyes don't go to him. They lock on mine.

"I thought I'd have to drag you away from the office myself." He strides toward her and presses a kiss to her cheek.

Casual.

Effortless.

Natural.

I hate how easy it looks.

I hate how much I want to do the same.

"We took care of it for you," the older woman says.

"Thanks, Ms. Thomas." They briefly embrace, and it's obvious Joshua feels comfortable around Claire's family.

"I keep telling her there are more important things than work, but she won't listen to me."

"I'll try to talk some sense into her." Joshua winks at Claire's mother, then looks back at me. "Ms. Thomas, I'd like to introduce you to my father, Declan Hart. Declan, this is Claire's mother, Judy."

"Nice to meet you." I shake her hand, doing my best to look like the man I usually am. Controlled. Polite. Unaffected.

"And you remember Claire, of course," Joshua says.

I shift my gaze back to Claire. "Of course," I reply softly, extending my hand toward her, although I know I shouldn't.

It doesn't matter that our hands are covered in gloves. The second I feel her touch, warmth spreads through me. It reminds me of feeling her hands pull at my hair. Her nails digging into my back. Her skin slick with sweat as we both succumbed to our urges.

"It's good to see you again, Declan," she says, her voice careful. Measured.

"You, as well."

"This is my sister, Genevieve," Claire states, pulling her hand from mine. "You're staying in her fiancé's townhouse right now."

"I've heard a lot about you," Genevieve offers with a sly smile as we shake hands.

Claire gives her sister a gentle jab, making me think she's heard more than she should have.

I notice her mother look between them, her brow furrowed in curiosity. Thankfully, the sound of a marching band playing "Jingle Bells" cuts through, and everyone's attention shifts to the approaching parade.

"Shall we?" Joshua looks at Claire, who nods.

He places a hand on her back and steers her toward the railing.

I join them, watching as the parade winds down Main Street. But my focus isn't really on the marching bands or the floats. Instead, I look at all the happy couples embracing in the cold, and an ache squeezes my chest.

I've spent most of my adult life living in cities. Walked by couples holding hands or embracing. It never bothered me before. Never caused this yearning deep inside of me.

That was before I met Claire. Now, I want nothing more than to pull her close. Wrap her in my arms. Press soft kisses to her hair.

But I can't do that.

Because she's the one person I can never have.

And I'm starting to think she's ruined me for any other woman.

TWENTY-NINE

Claire

The rooftop glows with strings of white lights, casting everything in a golden haze. Laughter rises above the hum of conversation while people sip champagne and mulled wine. The heat lamps buzz softly, warming the crisp December afternoon.

And then there's Declan.

He's across the terrace, sitting with Grandma Estelle. She's holding court as usual, gesturing wildly, her pearls bouncing against her chest with every emphatic word. I can't hear her, but I can almost guarantee she's telling him about whatever romance novel she's currently reading. And being the gentleman he is, his attention is glued to her.

Every time I sneak a glance, I find him already

watching me. He doesn't linger long, but even the shortest flicker of his gaze leaves me flushed, my skin prickling as though I've been caught doing something illicit.

This is the first time we've been in public together since we started…whatever this is. I hate how much my body aches for him right now. How badly I want to brush my fingers against the rough shadow of his jaw. How much I want to tuck myself against his side and surround myself in his warmth.

I knew what this was when we started down this path. Casual. Temporary. Something we could contain.

Something we could control.

But being this close and not being able to touch him feels like a cruel punishment I wasn't prepared for.

A burst of his laughter carries across the terrace, deep and rich, sliding under my skin like a secret touch. I wrap my fingers tighter around the stem of my champagne flute, forcing myself to take a sip and act as if I'm not unraveling from the mere sound of his deep chuckle.

"Mind if I join you?"

I snap my head up as my mom approaches with a glass of champagne.

"Of course." I slide over on the couch to make

room. She lowers herself beside me and tilts her flute toward me.

"To you finally taking a little time off. It's long overdue."

"Cheers," I murmur, clinking my glass with hers.

We sip in silence. On the surface, it's comfortable. I've always had a great relationship with my mother. Which is why I can't shake the feeling she didn't come over here just to keep me company.

I focus on the bubbles fizzing in my glass. On the flames in the fire pit in front of us. Anything but the man sitting mere feet away.

But it's like my body doesn't want to listen to reason, my eyes finding his once more. And when he notices me watching him, his mouth curves into a devilish smile he reserves just for me, scorching every inch of me from the inside out.

Who needs a fire pit when Declan Hart is mere feet away?

"So…," my mother begins, reminding me she's right beside me, "how long have you been sleeping with Joshua's father?"

I choke on my champagne, sputtering so loudly a few people glance our way, including Declan. But I purposefully avoid looking at him.

"Excuse me?" I manage once my coughing fit subsides.

Her expression is maddeningly calm, eyes sharp, lips twitching like she already knows the answer.

"That's him, isn't it?" she presses. "The one you had a sexual awakening with in Boston?"

"I didn't have a sexual awakening in Boston. I—"

She holds up a hand, cutting me off with the kind of authority only a mother can wield. "Claire. Please. You might think you can hide things from me, but you can't. I knew when you got your first period. During a volleyball game in seventh grade. I knew when you kissed a boy for the first time. Joshua, as practice, which was a mistake."

"Mom...," I groan, but it's useless.

"I knew when you had sex for the first time... Again with Joshua. Again as practice. Again it was a mistake."

I bury my face in my hands, wishing the world would just swallow me up so I can avoid having this conversation with my mother. But she's never been the type of mom to avoid difficult topics. If anything, she's always been the type of mother to blaze head first into them.

"I also know you smoked weed for the first time at your senior prom, and you got drunk for the first time during a party at McGregor's farm the summer before senior year." She takes a leisurely sip of champagne, her eyes never leaving mine. "So I'll ask again.

How long have you been sleeping with Joshua's father?"

My pulse pounds in my ears, the sound deafening. Declan's laughter cuts across the terrace again, and like one of Pavlov's dogs, I glance his way. I try to play it off, pretend to take in everything going on at the party, but when I return my attention to my mother, she smirks at me with a knowing gleam.

"I'm going to guess a few weeks. You definitely have that honeymoon-phase glow. When it's still new and exciting."

I part my lips to argue yet again that she's wrong, but it's useless.

"He *is* the guy from Boston," I finally admit on a long exhale.

"I knew it! I told you I sensed a change in your aura."

"I had no idea who he was." I ignore her remark, not in the right head space to talk to my mom about my supposed "sexual awakening." I doubt I'll ever be.

"He was just an attractive older man who was also stranded in the city. I didn't think I'd ever see him again. Until I went to dinner with Joshua to meet his father..."

"That must have been some dinner."

"You have no idea." I laugh under my breath. "When I learned who he was, we agreed it would be best to pretend that night never happened. But then he moved into Finn's townhouse, and we kept running into each other. And each time, it became harder to stay away."

"I can see that," she says without a hint of judgment. "There's obviously quite an intense connection between you. I can feel the vibration between you two."

I quickly shake my head. "It's not like that." I glance over my shoulder to make sure no one's listening in on our conversation. Then I whisper, "We're just having some fun while he's in town. I know it can't go anywhere. We both do. Hell, we probably shouldn't even be doing what we are, all things considered."

"And you're okay with that?"

"He lives on the other side of the country." I lean closer. "Plus, he's Joshua's father."

She studies me for a long moment, her analytical eyes raking over me in a way that completely unsettles me. "Is that a reason? Or an excuse?"

I open my mouth, ready to argue, but she places her hand over mine, cutting me off.

"Claire," she says softly, but with weight. "I love you with all my heart. But I also know you. You want to be accepted, so much so that you'll settle for less than you deserve if it means keeping the peace. You're a lot like me in that regard. You'd rather accept pieces of someone rather than nothing at all."

"That's not true."

She raises a single disbelieving eyebrow.

"I did that with your sperm donor," she continues. "Convinced myself scraps were enough. That pieces of a man were better than none at all. I don't regret it, because it gave me you and your sister. But now I know I deserved more. Just like you do."

"I don't want more."

"Is that *really* how you feel? Or are you only saying it because it's the only way you think you can have him?"

"I—"

"You're an adult," she says, giving my hand a squeeze. "I won't tell you what to do. That's never been my style. But I've been exactly where you are. If you want more, demand it. Don't accept less than you deserve. Not from anyone. Not even a man who looks as good in a suit as he does. It's probably why Grandma Estelle has essentially kidnapped him. You know how much she loves…what does she call it?"

"Suit porn," I answer.

"That's right!" She claps her hands. "Suit porn. And there is definitely some incredible suit porn going on with that man."

"He also has some incredible sweater porn," I add with a giggle.

"I bet he does." She playfully waggles her brows. Then her expression grows serious once more. "But none of that matters if he's not willing to give you what you deserve."

I push out a long sigh. "I appreciate your concern, Mom. But I promise. I'm okay with our arrangement." I give her a sincere smile, but my words lack any hint of conviction.

And from the look in her eyes, I know she hears it, too.

THIRTY

Claire

The cursor blinks back at me from the spreadsheet, taunting me with all the work I need to do.

I scan the endless cells of numbers and letters, the mountain of files on my desk, the sticky notes curling at the edges with half-scribbled reminders. This week is packed with activities — carolers, carriage rides, cookie-decorating contests, and live music nearly every night. It should feel exhilarating. Instead, my head is in a fog.

Because all I can think about is Declan.

Worse, all I can hear are my mother's words from the other day. How she's worried I'm settling for pieces because I'm too scared to ask for more.

She's wrong. She *has* to be. This thing with Declan isn't like that. I knew what this was when I let myself fall into his bed. This isn't a fairy tale. This is two consenting adults finding an outlet for a few weeks. Nothing more.

But if that's the case, why am I still sitting in my office at 12:30 on a Monday, staring at my monitor, instead of spending my lunch with him? Why am I dragging my feet? Can it be because maybe, just maybe, there might be some truth to what my mom said and seeing him again might force me to admit it?

The thought has me shoving back from my desk like it's caught fire.

I refuse to let my mother get under my skin. She's just meddling in my social life now that Genevieve has found her happily ever after. Despite what she wants to believe, I'm perfectly happy with the pieces Declan's been giving me this past week. Especially when those pieces result in more mind-blowing orgasms than I thought possible.

I don't want more.

I don't *need* more.

I barely have a chance to close the back door to Declan's townhouse before he's sweeping me into his arms, his mouth hot and demanding as it claims mine.

His hand fists my hair, and he yanks my head back to deepen the kiss, to take more.

"I've been wanting to do that since Saturday," he growls against my lips, his voice low and rough. "Hell, since Friday. Since you walked out my door."

His lips slam against mine again, greedy and punishing, like he's been starving and I'm the only thing that can satisfy him.

"Do you have any idea how difficult it was to be so close to you and not be able to touch you? Kiss you? Fuck you?"

He nips at my neck, his hands desperately pushing my coat down my arms.

"I hated it, Claire. So damn much."

"I hated it too," I whisper, clawing at his belt buckle, frantic to feel his skin beneath my hands.

His answering groan vibrates through my chest. "It didn't help that I knew I'd have to wait until today to have you again. It was only two days, but it felt like a fucking lifetime."

I hate how much I like the raw vulnerability in his words.

I hate how much I want to believe him.

Worse, I hate how much I want him to keep saying things like this.

"I'm here now." I give him a flirtatious smirk. "So you can make up for lost time."

"And I plan on it."

We stumble toward the bedroom, leaving a trail of discarded clothing like breadcrumbs.

My dress.

His shirt.

My shoes.

His hands never stop roaming. Never stop claiming. As if he's terrified I'll disappear the second he stops touching me.

By the time my back hits the mattress, I'm panting, flushed, aching. His eyes darken as they rake up and down my body like a predator stalking its prey. And like an untamed beast, his attack is brutal as he thrusts into me in one hard, punishing stroke that steals the breath from my lungs.

The world narrows to the sound of our bodies colliding in a raw, feral rhythm that feels like he's carving his name into my bones. It's rough. It's desperate. It's pure need.

Yet hidden beneath the animalistic frenzy is something else. Something softer. Something that feels frighteningly close to worship. The way he circles his hips. The way he presses a kiss to my neck. The way he takes my hands in his, linking our fingers together. It makes me feel wanted. Cherished. Craved.

No one has ever made me feel like this.

It's a terrifying thought.

What if my mom's right? Am I only pretending

I'm content with scraps because I'm scared of asking for more?

Because I don't think I'm worth it?

Because I'd rather accept pieces than be left with nothing?

Declan slams into me harder, faster, erasing every shred of doubt and scattering it like snowflakes in the wind. For a few blissful seconds, he succeeds, his punishing thrusts the reminder I need of who we are. Of what makes us work. Why complicate things unnecessarily?

"Goddamn, you feel good," he grunts. "Like you were made for me."

He lifts a leg, propping it over his shoulder and plunging so deep I cry out. He leans closer, his eyes wild, his breath warming my skin.

"Say you're mine, Claire."

I'm not. I can never be. But how can I deny him when he looks at me like my words are oxygen, the only thing keeping him alive?

"I'm yours, Declan."

He closes his eyes, relief etched across his face, before crushing his mouth against mine. He pounds into me with ruthless abandon, each thrust propelling me higher. Each touch igniting a war I'll never win.

"Give it to me, Claire," he rasps. "Let me feel what only I can do to you. Don't deny me. Not now. Not this."

His plea undoes me, and I break for him, utterly and completely. He joins me seconds later, his body convulsing, his roar ripping through the room, followed seconds later by a familiar voice.

"Declan? Are you here?"

Joshua.

My entire body turns cold.

Declan wrenches out of me like I've burned him, his eyes panicked. Grabbing my wrist, he yanks me up, dragging me across the room. "Get in the closet. Now."

"What? Just tell him—"

"Do it." His tone is harsh, desperate.

"My clothes—"

"I'll get them. Please, Claire. Just hide."

Something in his tone unsettles me. I've never seen him like this. So terrified. So anxious.

I stumble into his walk-in, my heart battering against my ribs. He tosses my clothes at me, then shuts the door.

I hate the way being shoved in here makes me feel. Like I'm unwelcome.

Like I'm a secret.

Isn't that what I am?

Isn't that all I wanted to be?

From the bathroom, water starts running fast and furious. Like Declan's jumped straight into the shower in a desperate attempt to wash me from every inch of him.

"Declan?" Joshua calls again, closer this time.

"I'm just finishing up a shower," Declan answers, his voice casual yet forced. "I'll be out in a minute."

"I can come back if it's not a good time. I grabbed sandwiches from the deli. Thought we could have lunch. If you're busy, I can head next door since it looks like Claire went home for lunch."

My whole body stiffens as panic races through me. The last thing either of us needs is Joshua going over to my place and not finding me there, despite my car being in the driveway.

"It's not a bad time at all," Declan says smoothly. "I'm happy you dropped by. I'll be right out."

The shower runs for a bit longer as I dress in complete darkness, every sound amplified. A few seconds after the water shuts off, the closet door opens. Declan stands in front of me, dripping wet, a towel slung low. His chest rises and falls as his eyes lock on mine.

I'm fully prepared for him to tell me we can't do this again. That this was too close. Too reckless.

Instead, he presses his forehead against mine. The scent of his body wash clings to his damp skin, filling my lungs.

"I'm so sorry," he whispers. "I gave him the code so he'd feel at home. I didn't think—"

"It's okay," I assure him, though I don't sound nearly as confident as I wish. "Go. I'll sneak out through the bathroom window."

He pulls back and meets my eyes. "You shouldn't have to."

"Do you have a better idea?"

His lips part, then he shakes his head. "No. I just… Damn it." He tugs at his hair, his frustration evident. "I'm sorry."

"It's okay. Really."

I slip past him and tiptoe toward the bathroom, climbing into the jacuzzi tub and pulling up the blinds. I'm about to crack open the window and pop out the screen when a hand on my wrist stops me.

"Let me make it up to you."

I pause, turning toward Declan. "How?"

"This weekend. We'll go somewhere. Tahoe, maybe. I'll get us a suite. Take you to dinner. We'll walk down the street holding hands, and I'll kiss you whenever the hell I want. No hiding. No interruptions."

My heart twists. I should say no. Should stop this before it tangles me up in a way I'll never be able to escape. But the picture he paints is tempting.

Too tempting.

Especially when I've fantasized about this exact thing since seeing him at the parade on Saturday and imagined what it would be like to be able to kiss and touch him without a single care for who might see us.

I could have that, if only for one night.

But we've proven time and again that one night is never enough. I'll want more. And more isn't in the cards for us.

Regardless, I can't find the strength to say no to him. I couldn't in Boston. I couldn't last week when he practically begged me to tell him to stop.

And I can't right now, either.

"Okay." I smile. "It's a date."

His entire expression lights up, and he clutches my face in his hands, touching a kiss to my lips.

"Thank you," he murmurs against my mouth.

Then he disappears into the bedroom, hastily dressing in a pair of jeans and a t-shirt before heading down the hallway and into the kitchen to spend time with his son.

As I watch him go, my mother's words echo in my head once more, louder than before.

Could she be right?

Is this all just another example of me settling for whatever pieces Declan is willing to give me because I'm worried he won't give me anything at all?

THIRTY-ONE

Claire

The streets glitter with Christmas lights, wreaths strung between lampposts, every shop window glowing with holiday-themed displays. Snow dusts the rooftops, and when the wind kicks up, flakes swirl around us like something out of a snow globe.

Declan's hand is warm around mine, his grip steady, reassuring, possessive in a way that makes me feel both safe and cherished. Each time his thumb strokes across my knuckles, a little shiver races through me, one I try to blame on the cold.

Every few steps, I catch him stealing a glance at me, as though he can't help himself. And every time, my lips curve into a smile that refuses to leave. My cheeks ache from it, but I don't care. There's a lightness in him tonight, as though some invisible burden has been lifted.

I feel it, too. For once, neither of us is looking over our shoulders, worried we'll be caught.

Tonight, we can finally be free.

Out of nowhere, he comes to an abrupt stop and tugs me against him, the sudden motion stealing my breath. Then he crashes his mouth down on mine, hot and fierce. My gut instinct is to push him away, remind him we can't do this in public. But then I remember. Here, we can.

Tourists skirt around us, boots crunching in the snow, someone whistling low as they pass. Declan doesn't notice, doesn't care. His only focus is me. His tongue sensually strokes mine, and I taste mint on his lips, the heat of him a stark contrast to the chilly night air.

He kisses me like I belong to him.

Even though I know I don't, a reckless part of me aches to.

When he finally pulls back, I'm dazed, my lips tingling.

"What was that for?" I exhale breathlessly.

His smile is pure sin, and it sends a jolt of need straight to my core. "Because I can. I like being able to kiss you whenever I want."

The words sink deeper than they should. I tell myself not to read into them. Not to let my heart twist them into promises he'll never be able to fulfill. But my heart never seems to listen when Declan's around.

We reach the restaurant, its windows glowing against the night. Inside, it's warm and intimate. Candles flicker on each table. Crystal glasses glint. Soft, ambient music plays in the background. The hostess leads us to a table by the window, where the lake glimmers dark and glassy beneath the mountains.

Declan sits across from me, his gaze never straying, his eyes raking over me like he's trying to memorize every feature.

"You look beautiful, Claire," he says, his voice low and husky.

Heat rushes to my cheeks. "No need to work your charms on me," I say to cut through the tension. "In case you've forgotten, I'm a sure bet tonight."

He takes my hand in his, bringing it up to his lips. Almost like he can't stop kissing or touching me.

"I can still tell you that you're beautiful. You're the most beautiful woman I've ever met."

I part my lips, on the brink of insisting that's precisely the sort of thing he *shouldn't* say. But the words die on my tongue.

I *want* to hear him call me beautiful. Want to box up his words and tuck them away somewhere safe so I can revisit this moment when I need to feel something good. Something honest. Something real.

"Thank you," I whisper.

Dinner passes in a haze. The food is exquisite, but it's secondary to the pull between us.

At first, I wasn't sure what to expect tonight. Up until now, most of our time together has been spent in the bedroom, both of us desperately trying to satisfy our cravings in the little time we could steal.

But tonight, we have the luxury of time and anonymity, giving us space to talk in a way we haven't before. We discuss our interests, the places we've been, the things we've wanted. He listens like every word I say matters. And I'm transfixed by every piece of his life he shares with me.

He tells me about law school. About how he got interested in civil rights. About how the military shaped him. I don't press him to talk too much about his childhood, since I know it might bring up difficult memories. I don't want to do anything to lose this version of Declan.

It reminds me of the man who approached me at a bar in Boston and offered to buy me a drink after chasing off a creep who refused to take no for an answer. I've missed that Declan.

At one point, he sits back, his eyes narrowing on me as if trying to solve a puzzle.

"I'm really enjoying this. More than I thought I would. Don't get me wrong," he adds quickly. "I love every second I spend with you in the bedroom. But being here with you, spending time with you fully clothed… I like it."

I arch a brow. "You sound surprised."

"Maybe a little." He laughs under his breath.

I swirl the red wine in my glass before taking a sip. "Why's that?"

"I'm not usually one to wine and dine a woman. Not like this."

"Too busy with work?"

He slowly shakes his head. "No desire. But with you…" His gaze darkens, locking onto mine.

"Yes?" I lean toward him.

"You make me want things I'm not supposed to."

My foolishly hopeful heart races. "Like what?"

"You."

I laugh nervously, trying to lighten the weight of his words. "You've already had me. More times than I can count."

He doesn't smile. Doesn't laugh. Doesn't look away. If anything, the intensity in his gaze deepens.

"I'm talking about more than just your body, Claire. And I have no business wanting more than that. Not when I'm incapable of giving you more in return."

"You don't give yourself enough credit," I whisper.

"It's true," he says firmly. "And I'm a selfish bastard for wanting to spend more time with you than

I deserve. But you're a goddamn drug. I don't know what I'm going to do when I leave here."

I open my mouth, on the brink of suggesting it doesn't have to end. But I swallow it down. If I only get this version of Declan for one night, I don't want to ruin it. Don't want to do or say anything to chase him away.

"I guess you'll just have to spend a lot of time in the shower, jerking off to the memory of me."

He chuckles, the low and rough sound warming me. "I guess so."

But as I take another sip of wine, my mother's voice echoes in my head, telling me I deserve more than scraps.

I shove the thought away, convincing myself this is fine. That this is enough.

But with every stolen glance, every laugh, every brush of his hand on mine, I begin to question whether it *is* enough. Begin to wonder what it would be like if this were real. If we weren't bound by time-lines and rules and the inevitable ending waiting for us.

If he were mine.

If I were his.

By the time we get back to the suite, I'm relieved.

At first, I thought I wanted this. Holding hands down snow-dusted streets. Heated glances across candlelight. Stolen kisses in the middle of the sidewalk, as if he couldn't hold back.

It was everything I'd secretly dreamed about.

But dreams come with consequences.

Because the whole time I kept thinking I could get used to this.

And that's dangerous.

When the door clicks shut behind us and we're back in the private world we know, I breathe easier. This I understand. This is safe. This is what we're built on.

Sex. Heat. Bodies. That's all this is. All it can be.

Except tonight, Declan isn't the man who presses me up against the nearest wall, rough and urgent. He isn't impatient, like he's been starving for me all day.

He's slow. Deliberate.

He slides my dress off my shoulders as if savoring every inch of skin revealed, pressing open-mouthed kisses along the curve of my neck. His hands glide down my body with a patience I've never seen in him.

When he lays me out on the bed and pushes inside of me, it's not filled with desperation or hunger. Instead, his motions have a kind of reverence I don't know what to do with. His hand slides down my arm, not to pin my wrist like usual, but to lace our fingers together. He holds me there, not restrained but tethered. Connected.

It terrifies me.

I close my eyes, needing to distance myself from him. From *this*.

"Don't," he rasps. "Look at me." His voice is low. Commanding.

I force my eyes open, and the sight of him nearly undoes me. His gaze is molten, fierce, threaded with something I don't dare name.

It's too much. Too raw. Too real.

But I can't look away.

"Declan," I whisper, the need inside me burning hotter and brighter until I'm trembling, on the verge of tears. "Please. Harder. Faster."

His grip tightens on my hands, his pace remaining slow and sensual.

"No," he growls softly. "Like this. I want to feel you this way. And I want you to feel me this way. Want you to feel everything."

And god help me, I do feel everything.

Every thrust.

Every kiss.

Every ragged breath.

It feels like he's cracking me open from the inside out, peeling away all the defenses I've built, all the walls I've sworn to keep between us.

I hate it.

I love it.

I want more of it.

I never want to feel it again.

Tears prick the back of my eyes, but I force them down, clinging to him like I'll drown if I let go.

This was supposed to be simple.

Pleasure, not emotions.

Sex, not love.

Temporary, not forever.

But tonight has changed everything.

Because now I can't keep pretending. I can't lie to myself anymore.

I've fallen for the one man I'm not supposed to love.

And the one man I can never have.

THIRTY-TWO

Claire

By the time I pull into the driveway of my townhouse the next afternoon, I'm grateful to be back in Sycamore Falls. This is what I need. To be somewhere familiar and put space between Declan and me. Distance always dulls sharp edges. Out of sight, out of mind. That's how it's supposed to work.

Except it doesn't.

Declan is still everywhere. In the ache between my legs. In the ghost of his fingers brushing against my skin. In the way my lips tingle whenever I replay the moment at the hotel door as we said goodbye, his mouth lingering on mine like letting me go was physically painful.

None of it felt like just sex.

None of it felt temporary.

And yet, that's all we are. All we're supposed to be.

But a part of me keeps wondering… *What if?*

Needing to silence that voice, I storm toward the kitchen cabinets and grab flour, sugar, and chocolate chips. Baking cookies should help. The process of mixing and measuring usually forces my mind to focus on something else.

But being in the kitchen reminds me of Declan. Of the night he barged in, eyes wild with fear as the smoke detector shrieked overhead, unbeknownst to me. How he gripped my face like he was scared I'd disappear if he let go.

My pulse quickens at the memory, heat flooding my face, and I stir the batter harder than necessary. As if I can beat his memory into silence.

"Look who's finally home."

I jolt at the sound of Dylan's voice. She breezes into the living room, unbuttoning her coat and tossing it across the couch.

"Where were you last night?" She waggles her brows and gives me a teasing smile.

But instead of giving her some half-hearted excuse, the question that's been gnawing at me for over a week spills out.

"Do you think I settle for pieces of people?"

Her light expression falls as she studies the tension

in my posture, the batter splattered on the counter, the too-tight grip I still have on the spatula.

"What do you mean by that?"

"Exactly what I said." I mix the batter with more urgency.

"Claire…" Dylan reaches out, steady as ever, and gently eases the bowl from me before I ruin the batter.

"Do I just accept whatever someone's willing to give me instead of demanding what I deserve?"

She doesn't answer right away. Instead, she allows my question to linger between us as she scoops perfectly sized portions onto the baking sheet. Finally, her eyes float to mine.

"Do you want me to tell you what you *want* to hear, or the truth?"

I huff out a laugh. "When have you ever *not* told me the truth, even when I didn't want to hear it?"

"Fair enough." She opens the oven and places the cookies inside. Then she leans against the counter opposite me, her gaze steady and unflinching. "You know I love you like a sister."

"As do I."

"But you do tend to put other people's needs before your own. And it's not because you're weak or a pushover," she adds quickly. "I've seen you stand your ground when it matters. Mostly in your job. But in relationships?" She shrugs. "You settle. You don't ask for more. You accept leftovers instead of demanding a meal of your own. Like with Joshua."

I straighten, furrowing my brow. "I didn't want more with Joshua. I was the one who ended…whatever we were."

"True, but how long did it take you to finally do that?"

I don't respond. I don't need to. She knows the answer. As do I.

It wasn't until Joshua proposed that I realized how deep I'd allowed myself to get. By that point, we'd been sleeping together for over five years. Sure, I'd dated other people on occasion, usually only when he was also dating someone, but it never went anywhere.

"How many times did you meet someone you liked but didn't pursue it because Joshua was going through a difficult breakup, or he was upset over his mom, or it was Tuesday?" Dylan continues. "You always put *his* needs ahead of your own. I love Joshua, but he took advantage of you. And you let him."

I close my eyes, unable to come up with any argument or explanation. Because she's right. I always everything to be there for Joshua. Hell, if he hadn't proposed, I may *still* be there for him.

"Let me ask you this," Dylan continues. "What do you want now?"

"I…" I shake my head, searching my brain. The

room is suddenly too warm, the scent of vanilla too overpowering. "I don't know."

"Is that the truth?" She arches a brow. "Or are you just saying that because you're worried it won't work out between you and Declan?"

I whip my head toward her. "What are you talking about? We're not—" I stammer. "I don't—"

"Save it." She smirks. "I know all about you two."

I'm speechless for several long moments before finally managing to ask, "How?"

"It didn't take much sleuthing." She tosses a handful of chocolate chips into her mouth. "A few days ago, I came home to grab some spices and saw your car in the driveway. But you weren't here." She leans in conspiratorially. "And let's just say…the walls in this townhouse aren't all that thick. Not thick enough to drown out you screaming Declan's name. He must have really been giving it to you good."

Heat scorches my cheeks, and I cover my face with both hands. "Oh, my god."

"That's exactly what you said that day, too. Except a lot louder." Dylan grins, entirely too smug. "I had a feeling something was going on between you two, especially when I stumbled on you guys outside the bathroom at the bar all those weeks ago. I knew your excuse about giving him ideas for Christmas presents for Joshua was bullshit, considering he was eye-fucking the shit out of you."

"He was not."

She silences me with a look. Then she heads to the island and climbs on a barstool, her chin propped in her hands.

"Now spill. And don't leave out a single detail."

I don't immediately say anything. But after last night, I need to talk to someone about it. And Dylan already knows. I may as well confide in her like I've wanted to since the beginning.

So instead of keeping the truth locked away, I look into my best friend's eyes and tell her everything… Boston. The incredible sex. Realizing too late who he was. The stolen glances. The smoke detector. The night we gave into our urges. Joshua almost catching us. Tahoe. The night that wasn't supposed to mean anything but somehow meant everything.

By the time I finish, the cookies are cooling on the counter and Dylan's scooping more batter onto the baking sheet.

"And now?" she asks after popping the next batch of cookies into the oven.

"What do you mean?"

"What do you want now?"

I chew my bottom lip. "That's the problem. I don't know."

"I think you do." She faces me, giving me a knowing look. "But you're scared to say it out loud because of what it might mean. Just say it, Claire. It's me. No one else is here. Tell me what you want."

My pulse hammers in my ears as I summon the strength to give voice to my needs for the first time. "Him. I want Declan. And not in the shadows. But he doesn't want the same thing. He—"

"You're doing it again," Dylan cautions.

"What?"

"Making excuses."

"But I told him—"

"Fuck whatever you may have told him. If you want more, demand more. You deserve more than scraps. More than pieces. You deserve everything. And if Declan isn't willing to give you that, if he's not willing to *fight* for you, regardless of the obstacles..." She shakes her head. "Then he doesn't deserve you, Claire. But you'll never know if you don't ask.

"*You've* changed your mind about what you want. Maybe he's done the same."

THIRTY-THREE

Declan

The cursor blinks on the screen in front of me, mocking me with its steady pulse. A stack of briefs sits untouched on the corner of my desk, red tabs marking every section I should have already reviewed. I should be buried in case law, pulling apart precedent, constructing arguments sharp enough to slice through steel.

Instead, I'm staring at a single word in the brief I've been working on for two hours and thinking about Claire.

Her laugh. Her mouth. The way she looked at me last week in Tahoe as if I was more than I am. More than my failings. More than the mistakes I've made.

It's maddening.

This was never supposed to happen.

A fling, yes. Temporary. Easy.

But the more time I spend with her, the more I've realized nothing about her is easy.

I lean back in my chair and scrub a hand down my face.

I know better.

I've *always* known better.

The truth is, I *crave* her. More than I seem to be able to control.

And that terrifies me.

For as long as I can remember, I've fought to maintain control over every aspect of my life. I *need* the control.

But with Claire, I feel like I'm losing all sense of control. I feel like I'm losing who I am. Or maybe who I *thought* I was.

My gaze falls on my phone tempting me from beside my laptop, and I grab it, navigating to my contacts. My thumb hovers over her name, as if reading it might summon her. I almost type out a text, inviting her over for lunch, but stop myself.

It's almost Christmas. Soon, I'll go back to D.C. Back to my solitary existence. Back to the way things have always been.

Maybe the best thing for me to do is put some distance between us.

But the idea of never seeing her again, never *touching* her again, hurts more than I want to admit.

I've had flings before. Casual, uncomplicated arrangements. Some lasted weeks. Some months. When they ended, I moved on without looking back. Never thought of them. Never craved them.

Never obsessed over them.

So why the hell can't I do the same with Claire?

I force myself to scroll past her name until I hit Joshua's. This is safer. Better. More appropriate. I should reach out to him instead. Ask him if he'd like to get together for lunch. Remind myself who Claire is to him…

Who she's supposed to be to me.

My fingers move over the keyboard as I type out a quick message, but before I can send it, the unmistakable sound of a door opening shatters the quiet.

And it's not the front door.

It's the back door.

The one Claire uses.

I don't hesitate. I jump to my feet and head into the kitchen, coming to a stop when my eyes fall on her, her hair tumbling loose around her shoulders, cheeks pink from the winter chill.

She hasn't stopped by on her lunch break since Joshua nearly walked in on us. We agreed it was better if we didn't. But that doesn't stop me from erasing the space between us and cupping her face in my hands.

"I was just thinking about you," I say hoarsely, my mouth skimming hers.

Her lips curve into a flirtatious smile. "What were you thinking about?"

"How I need to stop thinking about you. But I can't." I crush my mouth to hers, drinking her in like a dying man desperate for water.

She melts against me and, for a heartbeat, I let myself have her. Have *this*.

"Why do you need to stop thinking about me?"

Because the longer this goes on, the harder it will be to let her go

Because she deserves better.

Because I'm losing control.

Because of Joshua.

But I don't say any of those things. Instead, I take the easy way out.

"I'm going back to D.C. soon. And whatever this is will be over." My lips move against hers again, our tongues tangling in a dance they know so well at this point. But one I can't seem to get enough of.

"Maybe it doesn't have to be," she says when I break away.

I still, darting my eyes toward her. I drop my hand, taking a small step back. "What did you say?"

She straightens her spine, lifting her chin like she's bracing for impact. "I said maybe it doesn't have to be over. Maybe it doesn't have to end."

I run my fingers through my hair. "Claire…"

"I know I said I didn't want more. That I couldn't have more with you, not with who we are to each other."

"And that hasn't changed," I snap, sharper than I intended. "You're still my son's best friend. The girl he asked to marry him, for crying out loud. I shouldn't have touched you in the first place. Not once I knew the truth. I shouldn't *still* be touching you. But—"

"But you can't stop yourself. Because you feel this, too, don't you? This connection."

I narrow my gaze at her. "That still doesn't make this right. Nothing will."

"We can try to *make* it right. Joshua's a reasonable person. If we talked to him, were honest about the way we feel, I'm sure he'd eventually come around to the idea of us."

"Us?" The word rips from me like a curse. "You think there's an *us*?"

She flinches, obviously hurt by my words, but she doesn't back down.

"There could be."

"No, there can't, Claire. You said you knew what this was. Casual. Fun. No attachment. No *us*."

"I know what I said. But Tahoe made me realize I want more with you." She pauses for a beat and licks her lips, as if steeling herself. "I'm falling in love with you, Declan."

The ground drops out from under me, everything spinning out of control as I take another step back.

"No, you're not."

"Yes, I am." She moves toward me, not allowing me to escape this. "And I know you're falling for me, too."

"No, Claire. I'm not. I—"

"I felt it, Declan."

Her voice trembles, but she doesn't try to hide from me. Doesn't mask her emotions. Not like I do.

Instead, she lets me see this side of her. Her vulnerability. Her affection. Her…love?

"That night in Tahoe… That wasn't just sex. You made *love* to me."

Her words lance through me, hitting every part of me I've tried to keep buried. But it's impossible with her standing in front of me, forcing the memories of that night to play before me. How I took my time with her. How I wanted to savor every moan, every sigh, every quiver.

"Claire, please, I—"

"I get that this is scary." She grabs my hands in hers, grounding me to her instead of allowing me to flee. "I'm terrified, too. But I'm done running from things that scare me. I'm done settling for scraps because I'm too afraid to ask for what I deserve. And I want you. I want us. I know you do, too."

Her conviction tugs at something deep inside me.

Something I can't explain. Before I can think better of it, I grab her face in my hands and press my forehead to hers, breathing her in like oxygen.

"I…"

"Yes?" She inches her lips to mine.

"I…"

"Yes, Declan. Say yes."

"I…" I pull back, meeting her gaze as she pleads with me to finally take a leap of faith. "I can't." I quickly release my hold on her, averting my gaze.

"Can't?" Her eyes glisten with unshed tears. "Or won't?"

"What's the difference?"

"You're a lawyer. You know one word can change everything."

"Not this time," I rasp. "Not when the outcome is the same."

"And what outcome is that?" she asks, although she already knows the answer.

She's known from the beginning.

And I'm the asshole who gave her hope.

"I can't give you more than I already have. And not because of Joshua. Because of *me*. Because this is all I'm capable of," I manage to say through the ache in my throat. "I wish I could give you everything you deserve. But I just… I'm not that man. Not for you. Not for anyone. You're better off without me."

Silence hangs between us, thick and suffocating. I

expect for her to keep pushing. She doesn't. I see the second the fight goes out of her, the normal spark in her eyes disappearing in a heartbeat.

She turns from me and retreats toward the door. I have to physically fight the urge to reach out for her, my head at war with my heart.

Just as she touches her hand to the knob, she pauses, her eyes locking with mine one last time.

"I don't think you give yourself enough credit, Declan. You're a good man. And you deserve more than what you've allowed yourself to have. When will you stop depriving yourself of the happiness you deserve? The happiness your mother would have wanted you to know? When will you stop punishing yourself for something that wasn't your fault?"

Her words hit me harder than I expected.

But I don't answer. It can't change anything.

Instead, I push out a sigh and turn away, retreating into the bedroom so I don't have to watch her leave. So I won't call out to her and make her promises I'll only end up breaking in the long run.

Her footsteps echo through the townhouse, each one pulling at something raw and unhealed inside me. Then silence surrounds me. And it's the loudest silence I've ever experienced.

"I'm not sure I know how," I whisper to no one at all.

THIRTY-FOUR

Claire

The barn smells like cinnamon and nutmeg, the kind of cozy warmth that wraps around me like a sweater. Twinkle lights snake along the rafters, casting a golden glow over the long rows of baking stations for the first annual Holley Ridge Christmas Bake-Off.

It's chaos wrapped in holiday cheer — metal bowls clanging, mixers whirring, contestants cursing under their breath when their icing comes out too runny.

But I welcome the chaos.

Watching contestants build and decorate elaborate gingerbread houses keeps me busy. Keeps me distracted.

Keeps me from thinking about Declan.

At least it should.

But I still find myself drowning in the memory of him. His hands. His voice. The way he held me like he hated to let me go.

Except he *did* let me go.

When I got home from work the day I decided to hand him my heart, his car wasn't in the driveway. At first, I didn't think anything of it. Figured he was probably spending time with Joshua.

But the next morning, the driveway was still empty. And again the next night. I immediately knew something was wrong. Knew he'd left.

Joshua later confirmed my suspicion, mentioning Declan needed to get back to D.C. for a work emergency.

I knew better.

The work excuse was precisely that. An excuse. He left because of me. Because I wanted more.

No matter how many times I tell myself it's his loss, that I'm better off without someone who can't choose me, I still feel hollow inside. Like I'm not worth sticking around for.

"Who are you rooting for?"

I startle at the voice and turn as Joshua sidles up next to me, his hands shoved into his jacket pockets. He smells faintly of raw earth and pine, a sharp note against the syrupy sweetness of the barn.

"What's that?"

He nods toward the bakers, who are scrambling as the clock ticks down. "Who do you hope makes it to the final round?"

"Oh. Uh…" I clear my throat, scanning the row of contestants, most of them local bakers hoping to increase awareness of their business. "I like Jaxon. Anytime I post a clip of him on social media, our views skyrocket."

Joshua smirks. "Always the marketing brain at work."

"I can't help it." I shrug, trying to match his easy tone. "I see a speck of dirt and want to figure out a way to market it as artisanal holiday soil and make it go viral."

"And I love that about you." He chuckles, his eyes shining with affection.

Affection I don't deserve.

I turn my attention back to the contestants. One's piping buttercream onto his towering gingerbread castle. Another is caramelizing sugar with a torch. But despite the excitement surrounding me, all I can feel is Joshua's steady gaze on me.

"Have you decided what you're doing for Christmas?" I ask to cut through the tension mounting with every heartbeat.

"What do you mean?"

"Are you going to stay here or…spend it with your father?" The word catches in my throat.

Joshua's jaw works as he considers. "I'm not sure. Sycamore Falls is my home. But maybe going to D.C. isn't such a bad idea. That way I won't be surrounded by memories of Mom."

I give his arm a squeeze. "If you stay, you're always welcome at our house. You know that."

"Thanks." His expression softens, but his eyes don't leave me. I can feel the weight of them. Pressing. Studying. Scrutinizing.

I drop my hold on him, pretending to be consumed by the final seconds of the competition. But it's all just background to the heat of Joshua's stare.

"You love him, don't you?" he says softly after several protracted moments.

I whip my head toward him. "What are you talking about?"

"Declan," he replies simply. "My father. You're in love with him."

The air leaves my lungs in one harsh exhale. "I… What? Why would you—"

"You don't need to lie to me, Claire."

His tone is calm, steady, lacking even a hint of accusation. A contestant drops a bowl, and the crash echoes like a cymbal. Regardless of the unexpected sound, Joshua doesn't pull his attention away from me.

"You don't have to protect me from being hurt," he assures me. "It's okay. I mean, when I first suspected it, I didn't want to believe it. But then I saw the way you looked at him at the parade."

My heart aches. "Joshua, I…"

"And when I saw the way he looked at you?" He shakes his head. "I never looked at you that way. But he did. And that's what you deserve. I'm sorry I stood in your way of finding that for so long."

My eyes sting, and for a second, all the noise in the barn fades. It's just Joshua and me. Like it's been most of my life. He's always been there for me. Never judging. Never assuming. Just…there. After everything, he deserves the truth.

"We met in Boston," I rush out, the words leaving me before I can stop them. "Before I knew he was your father. When I met you for dinner and saw him sitting there, I thought I was imagining it, since I hadn't been able to stop thinking about him. But when it turned out to be him?" I blow out a long exhale. "It was definitely the shock of a lifetime."

"I can imagine." He laughs under his breath.

"He *really* wanted to focus on building a relationship with you, Joshua. I could tell how important it was to him. How scared he was over the idea of you hating him already. So we agreed to forget we ever spent the night together. Pretend it never happened."

"But you couldn't."

"No." My voice cracks. "At least, *I* couldn't. But Declan…" I trail off, struggling to find the words.

"What happened?"

"I wanted to change the rules. He didn't."

"Rules?"

"It was just supposed to be casual. No attachment. No feelings. Just…you know."

"Sex."

Heat floods my cheeks. I should feel mortified talking to him about sleeping with his dad. Part of me does. But Joshua has always had a way of making me feel comfortable. It's probably why he was the first boy I kissed. And the first boy I had sex with. He's always been my safe space. The one person I've never had to pretend around.

But there's never been that spark.

Not like with Declan.

"Exactly." I nod.

"But it became more for you," Joshua remarks.

"It did. And I'm sorry."

"What are you sorry about?"

"Everything," I say with a sigh. "Not telling you. Sneaking around. Breaking the rules and pushing for more. I'm the reason he went back to D.C. I'm the reason he abandoned you."

"No, Claire. You're not."

"Yes, I am."

"Listen to me." He grips my biceps and turns me toward him, his eyes blazing with conviction. "This is not on you. Just like you're not the reason your dipshit sperm donor left your mom. He *chose* to leave. Just like Declan did."

"But I pushed him. I asked for more. I asked for too much."

"There's no such thing as asking for too much when all you're asking for is what you deserve. If he's not willing to give it to you, then he's a fucking idiot."

The timer buzzes overhead, contestants rushing trays to the front, powdered sugar pluming like smoke. The barn hums with holiday cheer, but I crumble, sobbing into Joshua's chest.

"I ruined everything," I choke out, all the emotions I've kept inside for too long overflowing. "I knew how important finding your father was to you. I never wanted to come between you."

He cups my cheeks, pulling my eyes toward his. "It'll take a lot more than you screwing my dad to get rid of me."

Mortification surges, and I bury my face in his chest once more. "God, you make it sound so horrible."

His chuckle rumbles against me, steady, teasing. "I

can understand it. I mean, I got my good looks from somewhere."

I pull back and meet his eyes, staring at him for several long moments. Then laughter bubbles up, spilling out of me until I'm shaking.

It's the first time I've laughed in days.

"What did I do to deserve a friend like you?"

"As your mom would say, it was written in the stars."

I wipe at my cheeks, unable to stop smiling, an enormous weight lifting off me. "Thanks for being so cool about everything. For not hating me."

"I could never hate you," he assures me. "Plus, I'd be a hypocrite if I got upset with you over this."

I tilt my head. "Why do you say that?"

He drops his hold on me, shifting his weight from foot to foot. "Because I've sort of been seeing someone myself."

"Who? Rowan?"

I know he'd gone out a few times with Hayden's new nanny, but I didn't think anything came of it.

"No. Not Rowan. I sort of went out with her in the hopes I'd forget about this other person."

"Well, don't leave me hanging." I playfully nudge him, grateful to be back to the people we've always been to each other.

Before I slept with his father.

"Who is it?"

"Wynter Hayes. Well, I guess it's Wynter Patterson now."

I blink repeatedly, unsure what I'm more surprised about. That he has a thing for his one of his best friend's older sister who used to babysit both of us… Or that he has a thing for a married woman.

"What about her husband?"

"She left him after Thanksgiving. Apparently, he's been sleeping with his assistant. It's why she's here."

"Wow."

"Yeah." He pushes out a self-deprecating laugh. "So now you see why I'd be a hypocrite if I was upset with you over my dad. I get it."

I peer into the distance, processing all of this for a minute. This is the last thing I expected. Especially since Winter is ten years older than us. He always fawned over her when he was a kid. It was sort of pathetic. But I'm the last person to judge an age difference.

"I'm happy for you, Josh."

"It won't go anywhere. It's just a Christmas fling, more or less."

"Why do you say that?"

"Because of…life."

I nod, all too familiar with what he's talking about.

"Why don't you come over tonight?" he suggests after a beat. "I'll order tacos, crack open some growlers from Jude's brewery. We'll binge-watch baking shows and pretend we know what we're talking about. Throw around terms like isomalt and fondant and royal icing like pros. Take out minds off our fucked up love lives for a night."

"I'll have you know I *am* a pro. At *watching* baking shows. Not *actually* baking."

"I know." He flashes me a wink. "So what do you say? Baking show marathon? Like old times?"

I wrap my arms around him, grateful for his always-present patience and understanding.

"That sounds perfect."

THIRTY-FIVE

Declan

Snow falls in lazy spirals outside my D.C. townhouse, each flake glowing briefly under the street lamps before vanishing into the white-dusted street. The row of brownstones across from mine looks like it belongs on a Christmas card — garland looped over railings, candles flickering in windows, wreaths fat with ribbon and pine cones.

My place is the only one dark. Bare. A black hole in the middle of all that cheer.

The sound of voices drifts up from the sidewalk — neighbors stumbling home from a party, flushed with wine, laughing too loudly and humming bits of carols as if they can't hold all the happiness inside them. It's a reminder of what this time of year is supposed to represent. Togetherness. Celebration. Family.

Not for me.

I pour another glass of bourbon, the ice clinking in the silence. I'd invited Joshua to fly out for the holidays, but he claimed he had too much going on at work. I told him I understood, and I do. It's not the first Christmas I've spent alone. Hell, nearly every Christmas of my adult life has looked just like this — dark room, half-filled glass, silence for company.

I've always insisted I prefer it this way. That it's easier. Cleaner.

So why does the silence feel unbearable tonight?

Because I met someone who saw who I really am. Someone who slipped past every wall I built.

And what did I do? I shoved her away. Like the coward I am.

But what choice did I have? Claire is Joshua's friend. Hell, they were more than that once. That's reason enough. Isn't it?

Or is it just an excuse I've clung to because the truth is worse?

Joshua *is* reasonable, like Claire insisted. If we explained everything, if we told him how it happened, he'd eventually understand.

It wasn't about Joshua. It's *never* been about Joshua.

I've spent years convinced I don't deserve good

things. That I destroy whatever I touch, as my father loved to remind me every chance he got. It's probably why I pursued something with Claire. I didn't think there could be a future with her because of her relationship with Joshua. She was…safe.

Until she insisted she was willing to fight for me.

But I wasn't willing to fight for her.

The sound of the doorbell echoes through the quiet house, jolting me from my thoughts. I almost ignore it, but something in my gut tells me to answer it.

Setting my glass on the coffee table, I cross the hardwood floor and check the peephole. Snowflakes blur the edges of the figure standing there, but I recognize the stance instantly. Because it mirrors my own.

I swing the door open. "Joshua… What are—"

The punch comes fast, a sharp crack against my jaw. My head snaps to the side, the sting flaring hot before settling into a dull throb.

I rub my cheek, stunned. "What the hell was that for?"

His eyes blaze, his breath visible in the frigid air. "For Claire."

I stare at him for several long moments before pushing out a long exhale. I should have known this was coming.

"She told you about us."

"She didn't have to. I figured it out a while ago."

"You did?"

Joshua's mouth twists, part anger, part disbelief. "Pretty sure the entire damn town did."

"I—" I stammer, trying to come up with something to say in my defense.

I'm a lawyer, for crying out loud. I've made a career out of being persuasive.

With my own son, I'm drawing a blank. Probably because, deep down, I know I made a mistake.

Regardless, this isn't a conversation for the front stoop.

"Why don't you come in?"

He steps inside, snow still clinging to his coat. I take it from him, draping it over a nearby couch.

"Did you fly all the way out here just to punch me?" I grab an ice pack from the fridge and press it against the side of my face before returning to the living room. "If you did, I get it. I deserve it. I never meant to hurt you. When we met, I—"

He holds up a hand, cutting me off. "I know. Claire told me everything."

The shame presses heavy on my chest, and I drop my gaze to the floor. "I know it was wrong. I never should have… I just… I'm really sorry."

"I also didn't fly all this way out here for an apology. I understand why you didn't tell me. Why you both kept it quiet."

I lower the ice pack, tossing it onto the coffee table. "Then why—"

"I came here to tell you what a fucking idiot you are."

I blink, taken aback by his tone. Up until now, he's always been even tempered. Calm.

Not now.

"Women like Claire don't come around often," he continues, his tone hardening once more. "And you… You just let her go?"

"I didn't let her go." My voice rises, defensive. "I realized it went too far. That it would never work."

"Because of me?"

"I—"

"You're both adults. At least Claire is," he snaps, widening his stance. "When I said she told me everything, I meant *everything*. How she wanted more. How you refused to give it to her."

"Because she deserves more than I can give her!" The words roar out of me before I can stop them. My throat burns, my hands trembling as I drag them through my hair. "She deserves so much more than me. That's how much I care about her. How much I —" My voice cracks, the rest of my statement lodged in my chest.

Joshua tilts his head, his eyes sharp as they study me. "How much you love her?"

The word lands like a boulder in my throat.

Love.

I want to deny it, insist I haven't known Claire long enough to even think about loving her.

"I don't know if it's love." I hang my head and sink onto the couch. "I'm not sure if I know what love is anymore. Or *how* to love anyone the way she deserves. That's why I left. I had to."

Joshua sits beside me, silence stretching between us. The only sounds are the faint hum of the radiator and the muted carols drifting from a neighbor's speakers.

"She told me about your father," he says after several protracted moments. "How he made you feel. How he blamed you for your mother's death."

I close my eyes. "I'm sorry I didn't tell you."

He waves it off. "It's not exactly a heartwarming story. If I were in your shoes, I wouldn't want to bring it up. Wouldn't want to relive it." He leans forward, his elbows on his knees. "But I've also seen firsthand how that shit can stay with you. Take Claire, for instance."

"Claire?" My heart races at just the sound of her name.

He nods. "Her father walked out. Left her mother when she was pregnant with her. For the longest time, she blamed herself."

I nod, remembering her mentioning as much after I told her about my own father.

"She's gone all her life never asking anyone for more because she's worried about losing them," Joshua explains. "She's always put everyone else's needs before her own because she's worried if she doesn't, they'll leave her like her father did. So, the fact that she overcame her fear and asked *you* for more, put her heart on the line for you? That's huge. And you, the man who claims to care about her… You ran. Because you're a fucking coward."

The truth detonates inside me. My breath comes ragged, my face heating. I knew her father left. But I never realized how deep it went.

Claire, who has spent her whole life terrified of being left, offered me her heart. Overcame her fears for me. And I left her anyway. Just like her father.

"Fuck," I whisper, my voice breaking.

"I'm not going to sit here and tell you I can understand your thought process. I was raised by an amazing woman who made me feel loved every single day. I don't know what it's like to grow up with someone who made you feel worthless. But I do know this…" He looks at me, unflinching.

"You're not that man. I've seen who you are these past few weeks. You stayed in Sycamore Falls just so I wouldn't have to spend my first Christmas without my mom alone. Whether you want to admit it or not, that's what love is."

The words strike deeper than a punch. My chest feels tight. *Too* tight.

I didn't think I was capable of love. Didn't think I was deserving of being loved.

But if Claire's willing to overcome her fear, can't I do the same?

"So fuck what your father made you believe," Joshua continues. "Stop letting him control your life. If you want Claire, go after her. Prove you're different. That you're not the man your father made you think you are. But if you hurt her again?" His mouth hardens. "I'll make sure you regret it."

A small chuckle falls from my throat as I look upon my son with something that feels an awful lot like pride.

"I hope your mother realized what an amazing young man she raised before she passed."

"She knew."

I peer into his eyes, seeing pieces of myself in him. A part of me wonders how he would have turned out if things had been different. If I'd given his mother my number and she'd reached out about the pregnancy. I can't help but think he was better off without me. Or is that just my father speaking?

"What the hell do I do?" I rake a hand through my hair. "I was awful to her."

"Grovel," he answers without hesitation. "And

when you think you've groveled enough?" His grin sharpens. "Grovel more."

I lean back against the couch, the weight of his words settling in. For the first time since I watched Claire walk away, something sparks in my chest. Not certainty, but possibility.

Claire may slam the door in my face, and I wouldn't blame her.

But she took a risk on me.

It's my turn to take a risk on her.

THIRTY-SIX

Claire

Silver and gold streamers shimmer from the rafters of the Holley Ridge barn, glinting under the twinkle of thousands of fairy lights. A band plays an upbeat jazz tune, couples spinning in a blur of sequins and champagne, the room alive with celebration.

Laughter blends with the clinking of glasses, the energy and excitement growing more and more electric as the clock hanging over the bar ticks down to midnight.

And yet, all I can think about is him.

I've spent most of the night near the edge of the dance floor, pretending to enjoy myself while my gaze keeps drifting toward the doors. A ridiculous part of me can't help but hope that Declan will show up. That maybe I'll get that same climactic ending like in books and movies, and he'll rush in at the last second like Harry did for Sally.

But the clock keeps ticking. And there's no sign of Declan.

"Care for a dance?"

Joshua's voice breaks through the music. He looks handsome in his suit, his tie undone like he's halfway between relaxed and rakish.

"It looked like you were having fun with Maisie," I say, glancing past him toward one of our co-workers.

"She's not who I want to dance with," he replies with a sad smile, and I know he's thinking about Wynter. "Plus, you promised me one dance tonight. Since it's almost midnight, I'm here to collect." He extends his hand toward me.

I hesitate only a second before linking my fingers with his. His palm is warm, steady, familiar as he leads me to the dance floor.

We move together seamlessly, our steps practiced from all the Thursday night dance lessons we attended in this very barn. Regardless of the fact that he'd probably rather spend his Thursday night relaxing or watching TV, he was always there. Always willing, even though dancing wasn't his thing.

The thought makes my chest squeeze. Declan

would never do this with me. He'd never step out of his comfort zone for me. Not like Joshua.

I just wish I'd realized that sooner.

"You're thinking about him," Joshua whispers.

I tear my gaze to his, struggling to come up with a response. Something less awkward than admitting I was thinking about his father while dancing with him.

But I can't lie. Not to him.

Not when he knows me so well.

"I'm sorry."

"You have nothing to be sorry about."

"You say that, but I—"

He twirls me suddenly, the movement catching me off guard. Laughter escapes despite myself. When I land back against him, he nods toward an awkward couple a few feet away.

"What do you think their story is?"

I know what he's doing. He's trying to distract me from thinking about Declan by playing the game we do whenever we come to the barn for dance lessons. And right now, I could really use a distraction.

I follow Joshua's line of sight and study them.

The man looks like he's wearing a tux that's three sizes too small, his shoulders hunched, face red from exertion. The woman's expression reminds me of someone trying to win a ballroom dance competition. I've never seen a more mismatched couple.

Then again, I could probably say the same about Declan and me.

"Don't you recognize him?" I say in mock surprise.

"No. Who is he?"

I lean closer, dropping my voice. "That's Paul Bunyan the third."

Joshua laughs. "Paul Bunyan…the third?"

"Direct descendant of *the* Paul Bunyan. But it's a bit of a scandal."

"What is?"

"He doesn't like being a lumberjack. Instead, his dream has always been to be a ballroom dancer. It's how he met Esmerelda, who's well known on the professional ballroom circuit. She has secrets of her own, though."

"And what's that?" Joshua asks, lifting a brow.

"She comes from a long line of circus performers. Trapeze artists, to be precise. Except…"

"Let me guess. She's afraid of heights?"

"No. She's terrified of clowns. Which kind of limits your circus involvement. Why do you think she's doing everything she can to steer clear of all the red balloons? It reminds her too much of Pennywise."

Joshua throws his head back, laughing a full-belly laugh. I join him, grateful he knew exactly what I needed tonight.

"You are deranged."

"You asked," I shoot back, fighting a grin. "Okay. Your turn."

He blows out a long breath. "I have no idea how I'll top a ballroom dancing lumberjack and a circus performer with a phobia of clowns."

"I have faith in you."

He scans the room and points to an older couple swaying offbeat near the tree. The man keeps stepping on the woman's dress, and she keeps swatting his arm without missing a beat.

"That's clearly a retired jewel thief and the cop who spent his career trying to track her down. Fred and Ginger."

I choke on a laugh. "Is that right?"

"Yup. But the more he chased after her, the more intrigued he became. So much so that he didn't want their cat-and-mouse game to end. Neither did she. Although a part of her hoped he eventually *would* capture her so he could use his handcuffs on her." He playfully waggles his brows.

"Sounds like one of Grandma Estelle's spicy romance books."

"Don't worry. Their story isn't *that* depraved."

"So what happened? How did they get together?"

"She finally let him catch her on Christmas Eve, right under the mistletoe," he responds. "He thought he had won, but she slipped the handcuffs out of his pocket and shackled him instead. To his surprise, he learned she's a modern-day Robin Hood, stealing from the rich to give to the poor. They've since joined forces to use each of their unique skills to make sure greedy billionaires pay their fair share."

"I think I like Fred and Ginger. The world needs more people like them."

"It sure does."

He twirls me again, and when I land back in his arms, he leans closer. "Okay, last one. Over there."

He nods at a younger couple standing awkwardly at the edge of the dance floor. The guy is stiff as a board, the girl bouncing on her toes like she's dying for him to move.

"First date," he begins.

"Obviously," I agree. "But the reason he's barely moving is because he just realized he wore his roommate's pants by accident. And they're two sizes too small."

Joshua bursts out laughing, his hand tightening at my waist to keep me steady. "That explains why he hasn't taken a single step."

"Exactly. He's terrified the seams won't survive if he does."

The sound of our laughter carries through the rafters, drowning out the low hum of conversation, clinking glasses, and jazz music. I don't even care that people are looking at us. I needed this. Needed to laugh.

Needed to feel happy again.

"How do you always know exactly what I need?" I say with a sigh as we stop moving.

"Because I'm your friend."

I meet his eyes, wanting him to see the truth behind my words. "I'm so glad you are."

"And because I'm your friend, I also know you need this."

I furrow my brow. "What?"

He steps away, revealing a familiar figure lingering nearby.

Declan.

My heart thuds in my chest, a myriad of feelings twisting within, fighting for dominance.

"Happy New Year, Claire." Joshua leans in and presses a kiss to my cheek. Then he retreats, leaving me alone with Declan.

He's impossibly tall in a navy blue suit that fits like it was tailored to his body. The light catches the faint streaks of silver threading through his dark hair. But it's his eyes that pin me in place.

Stormy.

Intense.

Fixed entirely on me.

He extends a hand. "Dance with me."

"I didn't take you for the type of person who liked to dance," I respond.

"I'm not." His mouth tilts into a nervous smile. "And I'm probably going to step all over your feet."

"Then why do you want to dance with me?"

"Because *you* like to dance." His throat works as he swallows. "And I'm willing to make a complete fool of myself if that's what it takes."

"If that's what it takes for what?"

"For you to forgive me for being an ass."

The words slice through me.

Around us, the room seems to hush, the music softening to little more than a hum. I catch Joshua in my periphery, his eyes steady. Then he mouths, *Give him a chance.*

The irony almost undoes me. Joshua, my first everything, nudging me toward his father, the man I once foolishly imagined would be my last.

"Please, Claire." His voice drops, becoming raw.

"I deserve more than just a dance, Declan."

"I know. But you also deserve to be with someone who *will* dance with you whenever the mood strikes. So let me show I'm willing to be uncomfortable just for you."

I stare at him for several long seconds as a jazz rendition of "Everytime We Say Goodbye" plays in the background. The pleading look he gives me is unlike anything I've ever seen.

Despite my uncertainty, I slide my hand into his.

The moment his palm closes around mine,

warmth spreads through me, like that feeling of coming home after a long time away. He draws me close, guiding me along to the slow sway of the music. He moves with precision and confidence. Like he does with everything else in his life.

"I thought you had a work emergency," I say after several protracted moments of tense silence.

"I think we both know I didn't." His gaze never leaves mine. "Thankfully, my son flew out to D.C. and smacked some sense into me." He blows out a small laugh. "Or, more accurately, *punched* some sense into me." He works his jaw.

"Joshua *punched* you?" I ask in disbelief.

"I deserved it. Hell, I deserved more than that. I was an idiot. A fucking coward."

I try to look away, but he won't let me. His fingers touch my chin, tilting my head until his stormy eyes are all I can see.

"I thought I was protecting you. From me. From being with someone broken. But Joshua made a good point. I've been letting my father control me, even from the grave. In the process, I hurt the woman who means more to me than anyone ever has."

"Declan…"

He grips me tighter. "You scare me, Claire. You have since the moment we met. I knew you were different. Knew if I allowed myself, I could fall so damn hard for you. When I found out you were

Joshua's friend, a part of me was relieved. It meant you were off-limits. Except my heart didn't get the message." His eyes burn into mine. "I fell for you anyway."

My breath hitches. "You did?"

"Yes." His voice cracks, low and rough. "You make me feel things I didn't think I was capable of. That I didn't think I deserved. That's why I pushed you away. Not because I didn't want to be with you. But because I didn't think *I* was enough. Because I didn't want to disappoint you like I have everyone else in my life."

I part my lips to argue again, but he presses a finger to my lips, silencing me.

"I'd rather be scared with you than live another damn minute without you. So please, Claire. Tell me it's not too late. That there might still be an us."

A voice booms overhead, announcing one minute until midnight, but he doesn't flinch. Doesn't look away. He only waits. Raw. Stripped down. A man ready to shatter if I say no.

"You want there to be an us?"

"More than anything."

The ache in my chest swells, threatening to burst.

"Please, Claire. Give me another chance, and I promise to do everything I can to become the man you deserve."

"I'm not sure I can do that," I whisper, the crowd now at three seconds.

His shoulders drop, defeat flickering in his eyes. "I know I messed up. But I swear—"

"Because you already *are* the man I want."

His head jerks up, surprise flashing in his eyes.

Then he crashes his mouth against mine. The barn erupts in cheers as fireworks burst outside the frosted windows, everyone celebrating the beginning of a new year, but all I feel is Declan's mouth on mine. His kiss is raw, desperate, the kind that steals oxygen and gives it back all at once. My world curves and tilts in a myriad of different angles. Then, out of nowhere, it feels like it finally rights itself. Like this was always the way it was supposed to be.

When we finally pull apart, confetti rains down around us, gold and silver flecks catching in his dark hair.

"I won't ever let you settle for pieces again, Claire." He rests his forehead on mine, grabbing my hand and pressing it against his chest. "You have me. *All* of me."

"And you have all of me."

"I wouldn't want anything less."

His mouth claims mine again in another kiss. Not hidden. Not secret. But for the world to see.

I guess I got my fairytale ending after all.

THIRTY-SEVEN

Claire

Boston in November feels like déjà vu.

The hotel lobby glitters with the same chandeliers, the same polished marble floors, the same faint hum of holiday music creating a cozy ambience. Last year, I'd walked through these doors bracing myself for long, lonely nights. Filling every empty hour with work so I wouldn't notice what I was missing.

This year is different.

This year, I have him.

Even if Declan couldn't be here like he'd hoped.

Despite the challenges of a long-distance relationship, we've made it work over the past year. Thankfully, we're both able to work remotely at times, which allows us to see each other quite often. Declan even bought Finn's townhouse so he has a place to call home in Sycamore Falls. I know this arrangement can't go on forever. One day I'll have to move to D.C. if I want to be with Declan. But I'm enjoying what we have. And what we have is amazing.

As I make my way through the lobby after a long day of seminars, I glance toward the bar that changed everything. I'd planned to head straight to my room to get some sleep before my early morning flight to D.C. tomorrow. But since this is my last night in town, I let myself drift toward the bar.

The bartender greets me with a smile, and soon I'm sipping a glass of wine, the robust cabernet warming me. The air smells faintly of citrus peel and clove from the mulled wine being served. The comforting murmur of strangers swells around me, intermingling with laughter and clinking glasses.

Relaxing into my barstool, I pull out my phone and snap a photo of my wine, ensuring I capture the familiar background.

Then I send it to Declan.

ME:

Wish you were here.

He doesn't immediately reply. It's not surprising. He's buried in oral argument prep and warned me he'd be working late. All so he can devote his full attention to me the second my plane lands tomorrow morning.

I take another sip, idly scrolling social media, when movement catches my eye. I look up and my stomach sinks as the same creep from last year, who I've been avoiding all week at this conference, makes his way toward the bar.

Our eyes meet, and I look away, but it doesn't matter.

He still takes it as an invitation.

Apparently, his ability to read the room hasn't improved.

"Mind if I join you?" he asks, looming over me.

"I'd rather you didn't," I bite out.

He smirks. "I'll take my chances." He slides into the chair beside me.

"I was just leaving anyway." I start to stand, but his hand clamps around my wrist.

"Stay. I promise I don't bite." He licks his lips, raking his gaze down my body. "Unless you want me to."

I open my mouth to berate him when a loud voice thunders behind me.

"If you don't want me to break every bone in that hand, you'll let her go right now."

My head whips around, and I inhale a sharp breath.

Declan.

Dark suit, broad shoulders, fury carved into every line of his face.

The creep's grip loosens instantly, but that doesn't matter to Declan. He moves closer, looming large over him.

"I thought you learned your lesson last year."

"I— I was just being friendly," the man stammers.

"Didn't look that way to me." Declan's tone drops, low and dangerous. "Now apologize."

"I didn't—"

"I said…" Declan takes a deliberate step closer, "apologize."

Several tense beats stretch out as the entire bar watches the drama unfold.

Finally, the man mumbles, "Sorry."

Declan's eyes flick to me. "Is that good enough for you?"

I square my shoulders, heart hammering. "It'll do for now."

Declan gives a small nod, and the man takes that as his cue to leave. But before he can make it more than a few feet, Declan calls out, "One more thing."

The man faces him. "What's that?"

Declan reels back. The crack of knuckles against jaw echoes like a gunshot.

The man staggers, clutching his face. A few patrons cheer outright, the bartender shaking her head but grinning.

"About damn time," she mutters.

Declan doesn't even spare the man another glance. He wraps me in his arms, pressing a soft kiss to my lips.

"What are you doing here?" I ask. "I thought you were pulling an all-nighter."

"I wanted to surprise you." His mouth tips into a wicked smile. "It *is* our anniversary, after all. One year ago, you screamed my name for the first time."

I laugh breathlessly, still reeling from his unexpected presence. "And they say romance is dead."

He smiles, but when he looks at me, there's something else in his gaze. Something heavier.

"Let me pay and we can go up to my room. Maybe recreate that first night."

His hand tightens at my waist. "I'd love nothing more. But there's something I need to do first. Something I've been wanting to do for a while and was waiting for the right time. I wasn't sure when that would be, but now that I'm here again, I know this is it."

My brow furrows. "Right time for what?"

Before I have a chance to wrap my head around what he's doing, he drops to one knee.

In the middle of the crowded bar.

Gasps ripple through the room, and I almost forget how to breathe.

"One year ago today, I walked into this very bar,

feeling more lost than I ever had. I'd just learned I had an adult son, and I didn't know how to process it. Then I saw you. And I couldn't tear my eyes from you. I knew I'd regret it every day for the rest of my life if I didn't talk to you."

"I'm so glad you did," I manage to say through the lump in my throat.

"I never thought I'd be the kind of man to drop to one knee in a room full of strangers, but you make me want things I never thought I would. That I didn't think I deserved." His voice breaks before his expression lightens. "And not just because of all those cheesy Hallmark movies you force me to watch."

"Admit it. They've grown on you."

"Maybe a little." He flashes me an easy smile. "But they don't hold a candle to us. To what we have. It's better than any scripted ending. Because what we have is real. And I never want to stop experiencing this."

He reaches into his pocket and pulls out a small velvet box, flicking it open to reveal a stunning round-cut solitaire.

"I've spent my whole life running from love," he says, eyes locked to mine. "But I don't want to run anymore. I promise to keep surprising you. I promise never to make you feel alone again. I promise to kill every spider in your kitchen and warm your frozen feet in the middle of the night."

A flicker of humor curves his mouth before his voice deepens, growing tender. "Most of all, I promise to give you every single piece of me. Every day. So please, Claire. Will you marry me?"

The bar falls silent, everyone waiting.

And for once, I don't hesitate.

"Yes." My voice shakes, but the word is sure. "God, yes."

The cheer that explodes around us is deafening, but I barely hear it. Declan jumps to his feet as he slides the ring onto my finger, kissing me with such intensity my knees almost buckle.

"You have me," he whispers, resting his forehead against mine, his promise for me and me alone. "No pieces. No scraps. You own me, Claire. For the rest of my life."

I smile through my tears. "And you own me, Declan."

EPILOGUE

Declan

The house still carries a faint tang of new paint, though Claire swears it already smells like cinnamon and apple pie. Maybe she's right. Or maybe it's just her. She has a way of conjuring warmth where I used to see nothing but drywall and windows.

Tonight, the scent of fresh evergreen dominates, sap clinging to my fingers from wrestling the tree into its stand earlier. White lights curl around the branches, casting a soft glow in the living room. Shadows from the fire flicker across the walls, the crackle of burning wood mixing with the sound of Christmas music playing in the background.

Claire rummages through a giant plastic storage

container, carefully unwrapping tissue from an ornament like it's a rare keepsake. Joshua sits on the couch beside her, holding up a clay star with edges that look more chewed than sculpted.

"You still have this? When did we make these? First grade?"

"Second," she responds. "In art class."

"That's right. The teacher thought we'd make masterpieces. Instead, it looked like elves puked glitter all over the tree."

Claire laughs. "It sure did."

It should feel strange that my wife has such a long history with my son... A history that even predates me, but it doesn't. It's just a normal part of my life now. And I wouldn't have it any other way.

"Want to do the honors, Dad?" Joshua asks, holding the crooked star toward me.

Dad.

It still gets me every damn time. When he first said it, I had to walk out of the room just to get myself together. I didn't feel like I deserved that title.

But Claire reminded me of all the effort I've put into forming a relationship with Joshua over the past few years. While I may not have had a part to play in his younger years, considering I didn't even know he existed, from the moment I received those test results confirming him as my son, that's exactly how I've treated him.

Like a son.

He's one of the reasons I decided to leave D.C.

Claire was ready and willing to give up Sycamore Falls for me. But whenever I tried to picture her in D.C. full time, I couldn't.

Hell, *I'd* started having trouble picturing myself in D.C.

I finally realized that D.C. never was a home to me. It was a place to live. To hide. To forget.

Now I have a home with Claire. The quaint farmhouse we bought a few months ago is everything I never knew I needed.

Claire is everything I never knew I needed. And I'm glad Joshua finally smacked some sense into me to make me realize it.

"Big responsibility," I joke as I carefully hang the faded ornament on a branch right in the center, like it's the crown jewel.

"It looks perfect," Claire says softly as she admires the tree.

She's right. It doesn't matter that it leans a little to the right, or that it's cluttered with mismatched ornaments. It's a riot of color and memories, each ornament a piece of Claire she happily shares with me. Summers at camp. Her first Christmas at college. A chipped reindeer Grandma Estelle gave her when she was eight and obsessed with Rudolph.

"But I think it's missing something," Claire says after a beat.

"What's that?"

Claire and Joshua share a look, and I'm convinced they're about to pull out another ornament from their childhood.

Instead, Claire reaches for the side table and opens the drawer, producing a bundle of tissue paper. She hands it to me, and I unwrap it, expecting it to be another handcrafted ornament.

But it's not.

This one is smooth glass, expertly painted. The letters glint in gold script.

Our last Christmas with silent nights.

And below that… Two tiny footprints.

For a second, everything stills. The fire pops, the tree lights twinkle, but I can't seem to move. My entire world narrows to this ornament trembling between my fingers.

"You're…" My voice is rough, broken.

She nods, her eyes shining as she stands, sauntering toward me. "You're going to be a father. Again."

Joshua grins from ear to ear. "And I get to be the cool older brother."

Emotion crashes through me. Joy. Fear. Awe. So much so that my chest feels too full to hold everything inside it.

I pull her into my arms, my hand instinctively sliding over her stomach, filled with wonder over the prospect that our child is growing inside her at this very moment.

"Best Christmas gift ever," I manage to croak out.

Then I crush my lips to hers, overwhelmed with a myriad of emotions. When I pull back, I face the tree and place the ornament in a prominent place. Claire nestles against me, and I wrap an arm around Joshua, the three of us admiring our lopsided, over-decorated tree as a family.

It's not conventional. It's not neat or simple. But it's ours. And it's perfect.

Because what matters isn't *how* the pieces fit together.

Only that they do.

Thank you so much for reading *The One Night Stand Before Christmas*.

Not ready to leave Holley Ridge at Christmas just yet? Then you're in luck. Joshua has a story of his own… **The Trouble with Mistletoe**.

I did not come home for Christmas to fall for a younger man. But I didn't expect him.

Scan the code below to grab your copy.

Itching to know more about Rowan and her over-bearing boss, Hayden? Read *Tempted by the Nanny* today!

I'm the nanny for a grumpy single dad.
And the heart keeping me alive?
It belonged to his late wife.

Just scan the code below to grab your copy.

Thank you so much for taking the time to read this book. If you enjoyed it, please let your friends know by leaving a review so more people can fall in love with Claire and Declan.

the TROUBLE with MISTLETOE

I did not come home for Christmas to fall for a younger man.

I came home because my soon-to-be-ex-husband bought diamond earrings for his assistant.

Merry Christmas to me.

I expected snow.
I expected family.
I expected awkward questions.

I did not expect Joshua.

He used to be the sweet boy next door.

My brother's best friend.

The kid who followed me around like I hung the moon.

Except he's not a kid anymore.

He's six feet, four inches of confident, flannel-wearing temptation who looks at me like I'm the only gift he wants under the tree.

He says I'm not too old.
He says I'm not broken.
He says he's not a boy anymore.

But in a town this small and with my heart this bruised, wanting him feels like trouble.

And this Christmas I'm not sure I'm strong enough to resist him.

TEMPTED
by the
NANNY

***I'm the nanny for a grumpy single dad.
And the heart keeping me alive?
It belonged to his late wife.***

Working as a nanny for Dr. Hayden Lawrence was supposed to be simple. Keep my head down, take care of his adorable kids, and absolutely do not notice the way his rolled-up sleeves make me weak in the knees.

I'm sunshine.
He's a grumpy doctor.

I believe in saying yes to things that scare me.
He believes in control, order, and never loving again.

We are complete opposites.

But living together has a way of blurring lines.

Late-night talks in the kitchen.
Lingering touches when he hands me the baby.
The way his daughter wraps her arms around my
waist like I already belong.

Falling for him was never part of the plan.

Neither was telling him that the heart beating inside
my chest once belonged to his late wife.

And when he realizes my second chance at life began
with his worst nightmare, it could shatter the fragile
peace he's fought so hard to rebuild.

I'm not sure which is more terrifying… Losing him,
or asking him to gamble his heart on a future that's
anything but certain.

ACKNOWLEDGMENTS

Thank you so much for reading *The One Night Stand Before Christmas.* I hope you loved spending the holidays with Claire and Declan as much as I loved writing their story.

I'll be honest. When I first sat down to outline this book, I tried to fight it. My gut told me it was meant to be a forbidden, ex-boyfriend's father romance. And while I adore a good forbidden love story (especially when there's an age gap involved!), that's usually territory I save for my darker T.K. Leigh books.

But Claire and Declan had other ideas. It was as if they were standing beside me, arms crossed, saying, "You know exactly what kind of story this is supposed to be."

So I stopped fighting it. And I'm so glad I did.

Because their story turned out to be one of my

favorites — warm, emotional, and just the right amount of spicy to keep you cozy through those cold winter nights.

Before I dive into Hayden's book (yes, another forbidden age gap romance!), I want to take a moment to thank the incredible people who make these stories possible:

To my family, Stan and Harper Leigh. Thank you for your constant love, patience, and support. You're my anchor through every deadline and draft.

To my amazing PA, Melissa Crump. You keep me sane, organized, and on schedule, and I couldn't do this without you.

To my wonderful beta readers, Melissa, Stacy, and Vicky. Thank you for reading early, giving thoughtful feedback, and catching all the little things that make a story shine.

To my incredible admin team, Melissa and Vicky. You make sure the behind-the-scenes magic happens and keep our community running strong.

To my review team. Thank you for taking the time to read and share your thoughts. Every review helps new readers discover these stories, and I appreciate you more than you know.

To my reader group. Thank you for being the heart of this community. Your enthusiasm, humor, and love for these characters make all the long writing nights worth it.

And finally, to *you*. Thank you for picking up this book, for trusting me with your time and your heart, and for coming along on this holiday journey. Whether you've been reading my books for years or this is your first one, I'm so grateful you're here.

Until next time…

Love & peace,

~ Tracy Leigh

ABOUT *the* AUTHOR

Tracy Leigh is the spicy small town alter ego of USA Today Bestselling author T.K. Leigh. She lives outside of Raleigh with her husband, daughter, special needs rescue dog, and three cats.

When she's not penning her next small town romance filled with heat and heart, she can be found reading, spending time with her family, or planning her next escape to Hawaii.

facebook.com/tracyleighbooks

instagram.com/tkleigh

tiktok.com/@tracyleighauthor

bookbub.com/authors/t-k-leigh

pinterest.com/tkleighauthor

www.ingramcontent.com/pod-product-compliance
Lightning Source LLC
Chambersburg PA
CBHW011127190726
48289CB00012B/2935